THE BLOOMING
TREASURE MURDER

Sally Handley

To my sisters

Jane and Mary Ellen

CONTENTS

1 AN INVITATION

The enticing aroma of spaghetti sauce filled the kitchen. Holly clipped a leaf off the bay plant near the window and added it to the pot. She gave the sauce a stir, then rested the wooden spoon in the colorful ceramic spoon rest she'd brought back from her honeymoon in Tuscany. Though she was happy to be back home in her New Jersey kitchen, she missed cooking with the Manelli women at Nick's family vineyard in Caprilli.

As she turned down the burner on the stove to simmer, the phone rang. She smiled when she saw her sister Ivy's name on the caller ID screen.

"Hello, Ivy. How's everything in South Carolina?"

"Great. The weather's up in the 80's, my flower pots are in bloom and they're opening the swimming pool this week."

"I'm jealous. It's not that warm in New Jersey, but I do have something that will make you green with envy. I'm making spaghetti and meatballs today."

"Are you making homemade pasta?"

"Yep. By special request. I only make it on the weekend when Nick's home to help." Holly sat down at the table.

"He still hasn't retired?"

"No." Holly frowned. "When I bring up the subject, he just

smiles and says he's thinking about it."

"And what about you? Still enjoying teaching?"

"Well, I have to admit it was tough getting back into the groove after taking the Fall semester off for our trip to Italy. But I only taught two classes. So much better than the four I taught last winter." Holly lifted the lid on the stockpot and gave the sauce a stir.

"Your Spring semester ended this past week, didn't it?" Ivy asked.

"Yes." Holly put the spoon down, her eyes lighting up. "You want to come up for a visit?"

"Well …" Ivy hesitated.

Holly's expression shifted to one of concern. "Is something wrong?"

"No, no. I'm fine. It's just … did you get your mail yet today?"

Before she could answer, Nick came in through the back door, Lucky, their border collie, close behind. Nick held a colander full of lettuce he'd harvested from the garden.

"Nick, was the mail delivered yet? Ivy's on the line." She hit the speaker phone icon.

"Hi, Ivy," he called in the direction of the phone as he placed the colander in the sink.

Ivy replied with a cheery "Hi, Nick."

"I'll go check the mail right now." He headed through the hall to the front door.

"Why are you asking about the mail? Did you send me something?" Holly asked.

"No, but I want to know if you got the same invitation that I just got."

"Invitation? Is somebody in the family getting married?"

"Uh – no."

"You're going to make me guess? I hate when you do this." Holly's tone conveyed her impatience.

"Well, I kind of would rather you see for yourself."

Nick came back into the kitchen and placed a stack of mail on the table. He fished out the *Sports Illustrated*, sat down at the table and started to leaf through the magazine.

"Okay, what am I looking for?" Holly asked as she sorted through the stack. "Oh ..." She stopped and stared at the address label on a cream-colored envelope.

"Then you got it," Ivy said.

"What is it?" Holly continued to stare at the label.

"Just open it."

Holly tore at the envelope flap. After reading the contents, she said, "Well, this is the first invitation to a funeral service I've ever received."

Nick looked up. "Who died?"

"My Aunt Peg. She was our father's brother's wife, but we haven't been in touch with that side of the family since Uncle Tim passed away. When was that, Ivy?"

"At lease fifteen years ago," Ivy replied.

Holly frowned. "Our mother didn't get along with Aunt Peg."

"But you see it's not really a funeral service," Ivy's voice drew Holly's attention back to the invitation in her hand. "It's a memorial service."

"Nick, slide my laptop over here, please. I'm going to look for an obituary on the internet to find out when she died."

As she turned on the computer, Nick leaned toward the phone and smiled. "So, Ivy, we're having homemade pasta today."

"Yeah, I heard." Ivy said. "I'm jealous."

"And I just picked lettuce from the garden."

"Oh boy," Ivy giggled. "You're making my mouth water. Wish I were there."

"When you coming up for a visit?" he asked.

Before she could answer, Holly said. "I found it. Margaret Lowe died March 1st. Why do you think they waited until May to have a memorial service?"

"I wondered that too," Ivy replied. "But you need to look for another envelope in your mail – one from a law firm – Davis and Davis."

"Here it is," Nick said, handing the envelope to Holly.

Her mouth fell open as she read the contents. "Oh my God!"

"What?" Nick asked, alarmed at her reaction.

"We're invited to a reading of the will after the memorial service." She looked across the table at him. "Apparently, Aunt Peg left us something in her will. Why would she do that? I mean …"

"Holly," Ivy's disembodied voice interrupted. "Look at page two. Look who else is named a beneficiary of the will."

Holly quickly flipped to the second page. Her face lost all color. "I don't believe it."

"Do you think she'll actually be there?" Ivy asked.

"I – I just don't know." Slowly Holly moved her head from side to side.

"Who are you talking about?" Nick asked.

Holly sighed as her eyes met Nick's. "Fern. Our sister, Fern."

2 FAMILY HISTORY

Holly checked her rearview mirror and slid into the EZ Pass Lane at the Delaware Water Gap toll station.

"I don't remember the last time we drove through here," Ivy said staring up at the mountains.

"Unfortunately, I remember the last time I drove through here." Holly grimaced. "It was for Uncle Tim's funeral."

"Oh, right. I was sick and couldn't attend." Ivy glanced over at her sister. "That was a pretty awful experience for you, wasn't it?"

"More for Mom than me. Aunt Peg was such a witch to her."

"Well, it *was* her husband's funeral. She was grieving."

"Call it what you want," Holly jutted her chin forward, "she was a witch. She said awful things to Mom right there in the funeral parlor. We didn't even go to the repast after the church service."

Ivy looked through the windshield up at the sky. "Looks like rain."

"Yeah, they're predicting heavy rain later today. Let's hope we get to the hotel before it really comes down."

Ivy leaned back in her seat. "Why did Mom and Aunt Peg never get along?"

"Oh, it was all petty nonsense. Mom said Aunt Peg felt their mother-in-law favored our Mom."

"Grandma? I can't imagine that."

"You were too young to really know what was going on back then. Aunt Peg was a jealous person. She accused Grandma of doing more for Mom and for us. I remember one Christmas she blew her lid saying the gifts Grandma bought us were more expensive than the gifts she got."

Ivy's brow furrowed. "Then why would Aunt Peg include us in her will?"

"I don't know. This just doesn't sound right to me." A light mist clouded the windshield. "Great," Holly griped as she turned the windshield wipers on low. "I'm beginning to regret letting you talk me into making this trip."

"Oh, don't say that." Ivy's tone was pleading.

Holly shook her head. "You don't really think she's going to leave us anything of value, do you?"

"No, but ..."

"Wait a minute!" Holly interrupted. "Do you think she's going to leave us some item that will serve as an embarrassment to us or to Mom?"

Ivy sighed. "I don't know. Maybe Aunt Peg would be that mean, but do you think her daughter would agree to be part of anything like that?"

"Little Peggy?" Holly's mouth curled into an amused grin. "Funny how we always called her that. Never just Peggy – Little Peggy."

After passing a tractor trailer, Holly maneuvered the car back into the right lane. "You know she wrote me a few times, but I just never replied. After that scene at her father's funeral, I didn't want anything to do with that branch of the family."

"That's too bad. She was always nice to you and me. Remember when we came to visit, she'd take us to the little grocery store down the street and buy us penny candy."

Holly smiled. "She did do that, didn't she?"

"I think she was in awe of you. She always made sure you got first pick."

Holly's smile grew wider. "Yeah, I never understood that."

"Remember, back then she was an only child. One time she told me how lucky I was to have you for a big sister. You were older and she thought you were just so cool. Of course, she was shocked when I didn't agree."

Holly laughed. "Well, I suppose it will be nice to see her again."

"And what about …" Ivy bit her lip as she glanced sideways at her sister.

"Fern?" The smile gone, Holly shook her head. "I told you, just because her name is on that list doesn't mean she'll show up. She didn't come to Mom or Dad's funerals."

"I know, but …"

"But nothing." Holly's tone turned sharp. "Look, you know, I tried to find her. Whenever anyone told me they heard she was living here or there, I'd do research, find an address, and try writing her. But the letters always came back 'unknown at this address', so I finally just gave up."

"I'm not accusing you of anything. I know you tried everything you could to locate her when Mom died." Ivy sighed. "It's just -- I barely remember her. I was only six when she ran away. Funny how, over the years, you can't help but forget. Sometimes I think of her, and it's kind of a shock. I have a sister and have no idea where she is or what happened to her. It just doesn't seem right."

The windshield started to fog. Holly hit the defrost button and glanced over at Ivy. "Look, I know what you mean. I often wonder if she married the guy she ran off with – if they're still together. I sort of liked him and don't know what Mom and Dad had against him."

"Do you think if she had waited until she graduated and turned eighteen, they would have agreed to her marrying him?"

Holly shook her head slowly this time. "I honestly don't know." She again shot a quick glance at Ivy whose forlorn expression tugged at her heart. "Don't go getting your hopes up about Fern. If she didn't show up for Mom's funeral, I don't see why she'd show up for a memorial service for Aunt Peg."

"Maybe this time will be different. None of us is getting any younger. Maybe seeing our names on the letter from the lawyer will trigger something and make her want to see us."

Holly pursed her lips as the heavy rain began to hit the windshield. "Yeah, and maybe pigs will fly."

3 CHECK-IN

Ivy sat quietly for the rest of the trip, lost in her own thoughts. Holly focused on the highway as the downpour increased, reducing visibility. The driving rain persisted as she maneuvered the car down the windy strip of Route 309 leading to the Forester Hotel.

When they finally reached the turnoff road to the hotel, Holly looked skyward and said, "Thank Heaven." As they approached the hotel entrance, she looked over at Ivy. "How about I drop you at the door with the luggage? You can check us in while I go park."

Ivy just nodded in reply. After Holly pulled up under the hotel awning and helped get the luggage out of the trunk, she watched as her sister entered the front door of the hotel.

Why had she let Ivy talk her into coming here? Yes, she was happy for an opportunity to revisit their childhood haunts, but they could have done that some other time. And then it would be fun. Coming here for this memorial service was a mistake. She was sure of it. As she circled the parking lot, she wondered if the rain pelting the windshield was an omen for what lay ahead.

Finally, she found a spot and parked the car. Pulling the hood of her raincoat over her head, she made a dash to the hotel door. Inside she gave herself a shake allowing the drops of rain to drip onto the rubber floor mat. When she looked up, she saw a smiling Ivy standing in the middle of the lobby, engaged in conversation with a short, rather dowdy looking woman.

"Holly!" Ivy called out. "Look who came to greet us."

Holly stared for a minute as the woman turned in her direction. Little Peggy.

"Oomph!" Holly uttered as Peggy rushed over, threw her arms around her, squeezing tightly.

"Oh, it is so good to see you two!" Peggy squealed when she finally let go.

Though Peggy was a year younger than Ivy, Holly thought she looked ten years older. Her black, voluminous raincoat appeared to be wearing her. Threads of silver wound through her tightly permed hair. Round, tortoise-shell glasses gave her the appearance of a wise old owl.

"Good to see you too, Peggy." Holly said when her cousin finally released her. "I was so sorry to hear about your mother's passing."

Peggy frowned. "I just told Ivy that she had been ailing for a long time. Her end was actually a blessing." Peggy's expression quickly shifted to a bright smile. "It hasn't been easy, but I've begun to adjust to life without her. Tomorrow's service will be a celebration of her life. That's why I waited two months."

"Well, that's a wonderful way to look at things," Holly smiled back.

Peggy nodded. "I also just told Ivy that I'm glad I caught you before you checked in. I didn't have your cellphone numbers, so I called every hotel in the area to find out where you'd be staying." Peggy grinned. "I guess my invitation to come and stay at the house didn't reach you in time, but I really want the two of you to come and stay with me."

Holly shot a quick glance at Ivy. She had gotten the invitation but decided to ignore it. "Oh, Peggy, that's very kind, but we don't want to put you out."

"Put me out? Are you kidding?" Peggy smiled. "I'm all alone in that big old place now. There's plenty of room. And we have so much catching up to do. Oh, please say you'll come stay with me."

Holly smiled as she imagined Aunt Peg doing a slow roll in her grave. Before she could reply, the door of the hotel opened, and a gust of wind drew their attention to the entrance. A man in a khaki raincoat stepped inside and patted down his bushy, wind-blown hair. He stood a moment surveying the lobby.

"Peggy! There you are," he said as he walked over to join them.

"Don, I told you you didn't need to come out in this weather," Peggy chided as she helped straighten the collar of his coat. "Holly, Ivy, I don't know if you've ever met, but this is my brother Don." She patted his arm with an air of pride. "Don, these are my cousins, Holly and Ivy."

"Hello," Don said, making only brief eye contact.

"Nice to meet you, Don," Ivy said.

"I think we may have met once at someone's wedding or graduation party," Holly said. "Nice to see you again."

Don nodded, flashing them a weak smile. He leaned close to Peggy's ear. "I got a call from Ron. He …" Don paused, casting a quick glance at Holly and Ivy. "We need to talk." He tilted his head in the direction of the door.

Holly couldn't decide whether the expression on Little Peggy's face reflected fear or panic.

"Um — could you excuse us a minute," she said to the sisters as she took Don's arm and led him across the lobby.

"Who's Ron?" Ivy whispered.

"The other brother," Holly replied.

"Aunt Peg's sons with her second husband, right?"

"Right."

While Don headed to the door, Peggy scurried back over to where Holly and Ivy waited. Clearly distraught, but trying to appear cheerful, she forced a smile. "Something's come up. I'm sorry, but maybe it would be better if you did stay here tonight."

"Don't apologize, Peggy," Holly said. "We really are tired. The heavy rain slowed us down and made the drive difficult. The idea of getting into a car and driving somewhere in this weather is not at all appealing."

"Yes, Peggy. Don't worry about us. We'll see you tomorrow." Ivy gave her a reassuring pat on the shoulder.

"Thanks, girls. I'll see you at the memorial service." Peggy turned and moved quickly to where Don waited for her at the door.

"What do you think that was all about?" Ivy asked as they watched the pair exit into the pouring rain.

"I don't think I want to know." Holly picked up her suitcase and headed to the check-in desk.

4 STEPBROTHERS

"That all happened so fast, I didn't get a chance to ask Peggy about Fern," Ivy said as she hung her raincoat in the closet.

"I'd like to hang up my suit. Are there enough hangers?" Holly asked ignoring Ivy's comment.

Ivy frowned. "Yes, there are plenty of hangers," she replied and walked back over to the bed where her overnight bag lay open. "So tell me about Don and Ron."

"Well, first of all, they're Peggy's stepbrothers. When Aunt Peg married Ronald Lowe, he already had the two boys. He adopted Peggy."

"Oh, so that's why her last name is Lowe and not Donnelly," Ivy said. "I wondered about that."

"Yeah, I guess Ronald Lowe was a pretty decent guy."

"Is Don older or younger than Ron?" Ivy asked.

"I think Don is about the same age as Peggy," Holly said as she hung her blazer over her slacks and placed them in the closet. "Ron's the oldest and he's a piece of work from what Aunt Mary told me."

Ivy sank down on the bed. "What do you mean?"

"Well, you see how mild-mannered Don is? Ron's the opposite. He's rude and arrogant — an all-around nasty guy."

Ivy frowned. "Peggy did appear — I don't know — unsettled when Don mentioned Ron had called."

"Yeah, I noticed that, too." Holly zipped her suitcase shut. "It wouldn't surprise me if he's threatening to do something spiteful, like contest the will."

"Do you know what his relationship with Aunt Peggy was like? Would she have cut him out of her will?"

Holly arched her left eyebrow. "I doubt it. Knowing what a venomous creature she was, I'd bet he was her favorite."

"Oh, Holly. Be serious."

"I am serious." Holly lifted her bag off the bed and dropped it in the corner. "As a matter of fact, I have a vague memory of Aunt Mary saying she'd run into Aunt Peg at some church function after she'd remarried. She introduced Ron as her son, not her stepson—kind of the way Little Peggy introduced Don as her brother, not her stepbrother. Aunt Mary said she seemed rather proud of him."

"Well, you can criticize Aunt Peg for a lot of things, but if she was a good stepmother, that says something positive about her. Don't you think?"

"You want to know what I think? I think we never should have …"

Ivy stood up. "Holly! Stop it." She dropped her overnight bag in the corner with a thud. "We're here. Let's make the best of it." She crossed the room and faced her sister, arms akimbo. "Besides, have you forgotten the Corporal Acts of Mercy? All that stuff about visiting the sick and burying the dead from catechism class. All the stuff you threw at me every time you strong-armed me into going to some wake or funeral for people I didn't even know!"

Holly squinted as she stared back at her sister. "Using my

THE BLOOMING TREASURE MURDER

own words against me, huh? Fine." She sank down on the bed in defeat. "I'm tired."

"I'm hungry." Ivy reached inside her handbag and pulled out a hairbrush.

Holly let out a small laugh. "No surprise there. Let me call Nick and tell him we arrived safely. Then we can go eat at that restaurant downstairs."

"Great." Ivy finished with her hair and dropped the brush back in her bag. "I'm going to go down and check out the menu while you call. Give Nick my love."

As the door closed behind Ivy, Holly reached for her phone.

"Arrived safe and sound?" were Nick's first words.

"Safe and sound," Holly replied. "I miss you already."

"It's only been three hours since you left. We're apart longer than that when I go to work."

Holly sighed. "I know. This is different. This will be the first night we've been apart since we were married."

"And a little before that," he laughed. "How was the drive?"

"Godawful. It started pouring when we were in the Poconos and still hasn't let up."

"You're not going out again?"

"No, the hotel has a restaurant. Ivy already went to check out the menu. She sends her love by the way."

"You sound a little off," Nick said. "Something besides the weather bothering you?"

"Remember I told you I wouldn't have come here if Ivy hadn't insisted? Well, let me tell you what happened when we arrived."

Holly stretched out on the bed and recounted their meeting with Little Peggy and Don.

"Whatever's going on, don't let it get to you. Any news about Fern?"

"No, and it's killing me that Ivy is so hopeful she's going to be here. I know she has this happy reunion imagined, but she's going to be disappointed."

"Well, you'll be there for her when she is. Just go to the memorial service and the reading of the will tomorrow, then come back home. No matter how it goes, in twenty-four hours you'll be right back here with me and Lucky. She's keeping the bed warm for you."

Holly smiled. "I love you."

"I love you more," Nick replied. "Now go find your sister. I'm sure she's picked out her dessert already."

"Ah, you know her so well. See you tomorrow."

"Until tomorrow, *amore mio*."

Holly grinned as she disconnected the call and got up off the bed.

Nick's always right. Twenty-four hours and this will all be over. I'm silly to worry.

5 THE MEMORIAL SERVICE

"Wow!" Ivy said as they approached the entrance to the Hawzey Lake Country Club. "This place is huge. Were you ever here before?"

"No," Holly replied. "Remember, our family wasn't part of the Country Club set when we were kids."

"Aunt Peg really married up then."

"If they were members here, she sure did."

Holly held the door as Ivy stepped inside. A young woman in a black pantsuit approached them.

"Are you here for the Lowe Memorial Service?" she asked in a subdued voice.

"Yes." Ivy nodded.

With a graceful sweep of her arm, the greeter pointed to an arched passageway. "Right down that hallway to the grand ballroom."

"Thank you," Holly said, and the sisters headed across the gleaming marble floor in the direction she indicated.

Once inside the passageway, Ivy whispered. "Grand ballroom? I wonder how many people will be here."

Holly shrugged as they approached a sign that read "Margaret Lowe Memorial Service" with an arrow pointing left. When they made the turn, they saw a line of at least a dozen people up ahead. Beyond lay the entrance to the ballroom already filled with people.

"Well, I guess that answers your question."

As they moved forward, Holly spotted the reason for the line — a table with place cards. When they reached the table, Holly grabbed hers and Ivy's.

"Great," she said under her breath after she glanced at the card. "We're at Table One."

"Be nice," Ivy whispered in return.

Inside the ballroom, Ivy scanned the crowd. "Do you recognize anyone?"

"Not really," Holly replied. "I doubt I'd recognize any of these people even if they were from the old neighborhood. We haven't seen them in at least thirty years."

"Here you are!" Little Peggy came up from behind and squeezed between Holly and Ivy looping her arm through each of theirs. "Come. I'll show you where we're sitting."

Peggy had on a black, long-sleeve A-line dress at least one size too big and two inches too long for her small frame. A single strand of pearls graced her neck. She smiled at the people watching them as they walked to the front of the room, her chin tilted upward in what Holly felt was a sense of pride. Ivy was right. Whatever Aunt Peg's attitude was toward them, Little Peggy clearly felt affection for her and Ivy.

"Here we are," Peggy said, steering Holly and Ivy to the table nearest the podium. Two women, already seated at the table, appeared to be engaged in a serious discussion, which they hurriedly broke off as the threesome approached.

"Georgette, Beverly, meet my cousins, Holly and Ivy." Peggy couldn't hide her delight as she made the introduction.

"Georgette is Don's wife and Beverly is Ron's."

The two women stood up, and Georgette, a petite, strawberry blonde, smiled shyly and extended her hand to Holly first, then Ivy. "So nice to meet you. Peggy speaks so highly of you both."

A head taller than Georgette, Beverly's platinum blonde hair, was pulled back in a classic chignon. She flashed a pained expression as she also shook hands without saying a word.

"Here." Peggy pulled out a chair and motioned for Holly and Ivy to sit on either side of her. "I'm so sorry we didn't get to spend last evening together. I want you two right next to me so we can catch up," she said as she took a seat.

Georgette and Beverly both sat down as well. Holly noted they did not resume their conversation.

Ivy placed a hand on Peggy's forearm. "I didn't have a chance to ask you last night, but we noticed Fern's name on the list of heirs. Will she be here?"

"Well ..." Peggy began.

"Peggy." Don suddenly appeared at the table. "Sorry to interrupt," he said with a nod to Holly and Ivy. "Father McLaughlin wants a word with you."

"Oh," Peggy said, looking apologetically at Ivy. "I'll be right back."

Ivy just nodded as Peggy got up and followed Don to the ballroom entrance. She looked across the table at the sisters-in-law and flashed a brief smile. "Sorry about the loss of your mother-in-law," she said.

"Thank you." Georgette replied, bobbing her head slightly. "We're certainly going to miss her."

Holly noted that Beverly said nothing. Rather abruptly she stood up and left the table without so much as an "Excuse me".

Georgette frowned as she watched Beverly cross the room

and walk up to a rather burly man with a buzzcut, standing by himself. After a moment, Georgette turned back to Holly and Ivy, frowning. "That's Ron, over there. She's worried about him. He's not taking his mother's loss very well."

"Oh, that's understandable," Ivy said. "So how long have you and Don been married?"

As Ivy engaged Georgette in small talk, Holly kept her eyes on Ron and Beverly across the room. When Beverly put her hand on his shoulder, he pushed it off. A moment later, a young man approached the couple and blocked her view. Turning her attention back to Georgette, Holly couldn't help reflecting on the contrast between the sisters-in-law.

Though a tad shy at first, Georgette exhibited the social graces Beverly lacked. Or perhaps Beverly just didn't consider Holly and Ivy worthy of her attention. Like Peggy, Georgette had on an unadorned black dress. A single strand of grey costume jewelry beads and small gold earring studs were the only jewelry she wore.

On the other hand, Holly recognized the matching dress and jacket ensemble Beverly wore was an Albert Nippon design she'd seen in a Neiman Marcus catalogue. Her diamond earring studs were at least 2 karats each and Holly guessed the diamond necklace she wore was worth thousands. Diamonds, hard and icy, suited her personality.

Ivy and Georgette were still talking when Don returned to the table. He gave Georgette a gentle pat on the shoulder as he sat down in the chair beside her.

Next Beverly returned to her seat on the other side of Georgette followed by the younger man Holly had seen talking to her and Ron. She patted the chair beside her. "Come sit here, Ronnie."

Georgette appeared almost apologetic as she looked across at Holly and Ivy. "This is Ron and Beverly's son, Ronnie. Ronnie, these are …"

Georgette stopped as Ron approached the table and glared at Holly and Ivy.

"Ron," Don intervened. "These are Peggy's cousins, Holly and Ivy Donnelly."

Ron grunted as he dropped in the chair between his son and Holly. "I remember you," he said as he reached across the table and grabbed the breadbasket.

Holly watched as he touched several items in the basket before he selected one. Instead of passing the basket, he again reached across the table and dropped it in its original spot. Two mini-muffins bounced out and rolled a few inches before coming to a stop against the floral centerpiece.

"Good Morning, ladies and gentlemen."

Holly was grateful when she looked up and saw Little Peggy at the podium. The service was about to start, eliminating the need for small talk with Ron.

"Thank you all so much for being here as we remember my mother. Father McLaughlin will lead us all in prayer."

Ron pointed to his son. "Pass the butter."

6 THE AFTER SERVICE

"And so, in closing, all I can say is Margaret Lowe was a treasure. She will be missed."

Holly reached across Peggy's empty seat and gave Ivy's leg a gentle poke under the table as Hiram Thurston, President of the Hawzey Lake Country Club concluded his eulogy. Aunt Peg was a lot of things, but Holly could say with certainty, a treasure wasn't one of them. Ivy ignored her.

As the portly president stepped to the side, Peggy adjusted the microphone and began. "Thank you, Hiram. Kind words indeed. I know my mother is looking down on us right now, smiling. My brothers and I appreciate all of you being here to honor her. Thank you so much for all your kindness to our family, not just now, but throughout the years. God bless you all."

Ron popped up from his chair before she finished the last sentence. Without saying a word, he bustled off in the direction of the nearest exit. Beverly inhaled deeply, her jawline tense. She whispered something to her son and they both stood up. Beverly took her son's arm and followed Ron at a slower, more dignified pace.

"Hiram, I want you to meet my cousins, Holly and Ivy Donnelly," Peggy said as she walked him over to the table.

"Ladies." Hiram Thurston gave a slight bow in their direction.

"How do you do," Ivy said.

Holly just nodded, smiling as Hiram remained on the opposite side of the table, making no attempt to get close enough for a handshake. The expression "stuffed shirt" came to mind. She struggled to keep from laughing as she wondered how many of the male members of the Country Club were as ... the English teacher in her struggled to find the right adjective. *Stout.* Yes, that was the perfect word to describe Ron and Hiram.

"Nice eulogy, Hiram," Don said. "Mom would have enjoyed it."

Hiram let out a stiff, polite little laugh. "Well, I meant every word of it. You know I thought the world of your dear mother. Why her fundraising efforts as part of the women's auxiliary committee were ..."

"Great eulogy, Hiram." The President winced as the man offering the compliment tapped him on the back. "We're going to miss you when you retire."

Hiram's expression turned grim. "I'm not re ..."

The man quickly brushed past him and turned his attention to Peggy, taking her hand.

"Peggy, dear, you know how sorry I am for you at the loss of your mother," he said as he stroked her hand. "She was a wonderful woman."

Peggy grimaced. "Thank you, Fred. That's very kind of you."

Holly could see that Peggy tried to pull back her hand, but Fred was not letting go.

"Now if there's anything I can do for you — anything at all, you know I'm just a phone call away." Finally, releasing Peggy's hand, Fred turned his gaze to Holly and Ivy. "And who are these fine ladies?"

"They're my cousins, Fred," Peggy replied rather

brusquely.

Unlike Hiram, Fred quickly moved closer and extended his hand to Holly.

"How do you do? I'm Fred Locksley, Vice President of the Board of Trustees here at the Club," he said gazing into her eyes. "What a pleasure to meet you."

Fred's gangly physique blew Holly's *stout* theory. His ill-fitting suit was just a tad short in the sleeves, revealing too much shirt cuff. His hair was slicked back in the style worn by younger men, but on this guy the effect was less than flattering. This time the word *smarmy* popped into Holly's head and she struggled not to laugh for the second time today.

Amused, she watched as he repeated the greeting with Ivy. "*Enchanté*," he cooed as he gazed into her eyes. Was this guy for real? Did women fall for this unctuous come-on? Holly had to cover her mouth as she watched Ivy struggle not to wipe her hand in her napkin after the handshake.

Peggy gave her head a slight shake. "Fred, you'll have to excuse us please. We have to get going. Girls, come with me."

Fred reluctantly stepped back as Holly and Ivy got up. Peggy turned to Hiram, her expression softening. "Thank you again for all you've done for us."

"It was an honor ..." Hiram began.

"Mr. Thurston." The woman who greeted them in the front lobby seemed to appear out of nowhere. She stepped close to Hiram and spoke in a low tone. In a blatant attempt at eavesdropping, Fred edged so close that Hiram bumped into him when he turned back to face Peggy.

"Do you mind, Fred?" he said, unable to hide his annoyance. Pushing past Fred, he said, "Sorry, Peggy, but duty calls. I must go." He gave Peggy's arm a squeeze. "Don't be a stranger."

Hiram turned and followed the greeter to the ballroom

exit, Fred close on their heels.

"All right then." Peggy smiled at Holly and Ivy and pointed to her wristwatch. "It's time. Come with me. I've reserved a meeting room for us."

She took the sisters each by the arm and led them out of the ballroom. As most of the departing guests turned left at the end of the corridor in the direction of the lobby, Peggy turned to the right.

"Here we are. The Appalachian Room." Peggy reached for the doorknob.

Inside, a distinguished looking man sitting at a table in front of two rows of chairs looked up.

"Good morning, Charles," Peggy said. After introducing the Donnelly sisters to the lawyer, she asked, "Everything ready?"

"Everything's ready, Ms. Lowe," Charles answered, flashing a pleasant smile.

Holly thought if you looked up the word *lawyer* in the dictionary, Charles' picture would be the illustration. His dark hair was accented by some silver strands in just the right places. The crispest of white shirts contrasted perfectly with his navy-blue suit and red silk tie.

"Great." Peggy looked at Holly and Ivy and pointed to two chairs on her right. "Here, you two sit there."

"No one else is coming?" Ivy asked.

Holly could see the disappointment on Ivy's face as Peggy glanced at her watch.

"Shouldn't we wait for your brothers and their wives?" Holly asked.

Peggy darted a quick glance at the lawyer, then shook her head, smiling at Holly and Ivy. "No. The bequests to immediate family members were handled separately." She looked at her watch one more time, glanced at the door and finally dropped into her seat. "Well, I suppose we might as well start. Go ahead, Charles, begin," she said.

The lawyer opened the folder resting on the table in front of him. "The will of Margaret Lowe includes a unique provision …"

Charles stopped at the sound of the door opening. Everyone turned to see three women enter the room.

"I'm sorry, but this is a private meeting," Charles said as he got to his feet.

"We know." The oldest of the women faced him. "We're invited guests. I'm Fern Brennan and these are my daughters, Jasmine and Violet."

7 REUNION

Ivy jumped up and rushed over, throwing her arms around Fern. "Oh, I was so hoping you would be here."

Holly remained seated, watching as Fern grimaced at Ivy's embrace, her posture rigid. She did not return Ivy's hug. After a moment Ivy released Fern and without hesitation hugged each of Fern's daughters who appeared more receptive to Ivy's warm greeting than their mother.

Ivy took a step back and looked from one daughter to the other, then back again. "Oh, my goodness!" she exclaimed. Shaking her head in disbelief, she looked back to Holly and laughed, "Look, Holly. Our nieces. They're twins!"

Holly laughed in reply as she stood up. A grinning Peggy quickly took her by the arm and led her back to join the reunion. As they reached Fern, Holly stopped, the smile fading from her face.

"It's been a long time, Fern," she said. Fern frowned and just nodded in reply.

"Come, Holly." Ivy reached for her sister's arm, pulling her towards the twins. "Okay, okay — now which of you is Jasmine and which is Violet?" she asked.

"I'm Jasmine." The young woman dressed in a green pantsuit replied. Her brunette hair was pulled back in a ponytail. She wore a droll smile, appearing quite amused by Ivy.

"I'm Violet," The second sister replied. Dressed in a lilac man-tailored blouse and black pencil skirt, she appeared a tad more reserved than Jasmine, her smile more earnest.

"I'm your Aunt Ivy and this is your Aunt Holly." Ivy put her arm around her sister. "You know everyone asks us if we're twins."

Jasmine's left eyebrow arched. "I can see that."

Peggy stepped forward. "Girls, I hate to break up this moment, but why don't we all take a seat and let Charles finish. There will be plenty of time for catching up afterwards."

"C'mon," Holly tugged Ivy's arm. "Let's go sit down."

"Oh, all right." Ivy agreed with reluctance.

Peggy led them back to their seats. "Okay, Charles," she said, "let's begin again."

As the lawyer picked up where he left off, Holly was grateful for the chance to process her feelings. For so long, she had wondered what it would be like to see her older sister again. Fern's cold response to Ivy's warm reception was the scenario she feared. But what did Fern have against them? They were just little girls when she ran away. Holly had to admit she resented the fact that Fern never said good-bye, never responded to any of the letters she sent.

Holly's thoughts were interrupted when Fern sat forward in her seat and said, "Wait just a minute. You're saying we have to participate in some cockamamie treasure hunt to claim our inheritance. And we don't even know what the inheritance consists of. Did Aunt Peg lose her mind at the end?"

"Now, Fern," Peggy soothed. "Mom had her reasons ..."

"Stop, Peggy," Fern stood up. "I can't believe you lured me here for this nonsense. I'm not staying here one more minute."

She turned and headed to the door.

"Fern, please ..." Peggy begged, running after her.

As the pair disappeared through the door, Holly glanced across the aisle and caught Jasmine doing an eyeroll in her sister's direction. Violet appeared to sigh, grabbed her bag and followed in Fern and Peggy's wake.

Holly turned to the lawyer. "I'm sorry, but I sort of zoned out. Would you mind explaining what Fern is objecting to?"

The consummate professional, Charles nodded politely. "Mrs. Lowe has provided for each of you in her will. She stipulated, however, that you must participate in what she termed "A Trip Down Memory Lane" in order to claim your inheritance."

"And this trip down memory lane is a treasure hunt?" Holly's voice echoed a skepticism equal to Fern's.

"Yes," Charles confirmed.

"And how is this supposed to work?" Ivy asked, appearing more curious than skeptical.

"There are three riddles. The first I have here to be read to you today. The answer to this riddle will lead you to a second location. There you will find another riddle that will lead you to the third location. Once you have visited all three locations, your inheritance will be deposited in your bank accounts."

"Are we competing with each other?" Holly asked, her tone growing contentious.

"No, no," Charles swiftly replied. "This is to be a collaborative effort."

Suddenly, the back door opened, and Peggy stuck her head inside. "Charles, could I see you out here in the hallway, please?" she said.

Charles immediately got to his feet and met Peggy at the door.

As the door closed, Jasmine looked across at Holly and Ivy, the amused smile back on her face. "Aunt Peg was a real piece of work, wasn't she?"

Holly smiled as she nodded in reply.

8 THE FIRST RIDDLE

Of course, Ivy was the first to speak. "Oh, Jasmine. Forget Aunt Peg. Tell us about yourself. Until a few minutes ago, we didn't even know you existed."

Jasmine uncrossed her arms and her expression shifted to a more relaxed smile. "Well, I'm forty-years old and I'm a lawyer."

"A lawyer! That's wonderful." Ivy gushed. "Isn't it, Holly?"

"Yes," Holly agreed. "What area of law is your specialty?"

"I work for the District Attorney's office in Miami-Dade County."

Before Holly could react, the door opened.

A smiling Peggy was the first to re-enter the room. Violet, her arm around her mother, followed next. Charles returned to his seat behind the table in front.

Standing beside the table, Peggy began. "Okay. Now, although I know mother wished to keep the amount of your bequests secret until after the treasure hunt, after talking with Fern and consulting with Charles, we agree that is a bit unfair to you. So, I will tell you at the outset that upon completion of the treasure hunt, each of you will have deposited into your accounts the amount of $100,000."

Ivy gasped.

"You can't be serious," Holly scoffed. "Aunt Peg didn't even like us."

Peggy winced. "I assure you — she — I admit Mother was a difficult person, but she ..." Peggy's cheeks turned red. "Charles, please confirm the terms of the treasure hunt."

"I have been legal counsel to the Lowe family for more than twenty years. I assure you the terms of the bequest are exactly as Ms. Lowe has described them. The funds are in an escrow account to be disbursed upon completion of the treasure hunt."

"What if we don't solve the riddles and find this so-called treasure?" Jasmine asked. "Do we still get the money?"

"Yes," Charles replied. "As long as you make a good faith effort to solve the riddles and go to the locations specified, you will receive your inheritance. The only stipulation is that you must all agree to participate and you must work together as a group."

"Well, I'm in," Jasmine waggled her head, grinning. "A hundred thousand dollars will wipe out what's left of my student loans and leave me with enough for a down payment on a condo."

"Great," Peggy said. "And don't you worry. I have every confidence that you five ladies working together will solve the riddles. Now, Fern, Violet, you agreed to these conditions out in the hall. Isn't that right?"

Violet nodded and Fern sighed. "Just for the record, I'm only doing this for my daughters' sake."

Peggy nodded. "Holly? Ivy?"

"Is there a time limit on the treasure hunt?" Holly asked. "We can't stay here indefinitely until the riddles are solved. My husband's expecting us home this evening."

"The hunt ends Sunday afternoon," Peggy replied. "If you haven't found the treasure, all will be revealed then."

"What if we say no?" Holly narrowed her eyes. "Can Fern and her daughters complete the treasure hunt and split our share?"

"No," Peggy said firmly. "If one of you declines, the money goes to the Children's Hospital in Wilkes-Barre."

Ivy looked at Holly. "You know we have to do this."

Holly inhaled deeply and let out an audible sigh of defeat. "Okay, then. We're in."

With a gleeful smile, Peggy brought her hands together in front of her and fluttered them in a soundless applause. "This is just wonderful. Now, one more thing. You all are coming to stay at our house—my house. With eight bedrooms, there's no need for you to incur the cost of a hotel or meals out."

"Really, Peggy," Holly protested. "We're quite happy to stay at the hotel."

Peggy shook her head. "I insist. I won't take no for an answer," she said sternly. Her severe expression quickly turned into a smile. "After we finish here, we'll collect your belongings and get you checked out. Fern, you girls haven't checked in yet, right?"

Fern shook her head.

"Then it's settled." Making a swift pivot, Peggy said, "Charles, read us the first of the riddles, please."

As the lawyer opened a large green envelope, Holly whispered to Ivy, "She's more like her mother than I thought."

Ivy gave her a poke in the ribs and turned to face the lawyer.

Charles pulled out a small, green single sheet of paper and read, "Where Helios ends his daily chariot ride you will find a gift from Seshat."

9 PATRICK KEEFE

Out in the parking lot, Peggy turned to Fern. "The limo driver knows the way to the house." She wiggled excitedly like a puppy with a new toy. "We'll meet you there and get started working on the riddle."

As Fern, Jasmine and Violet headed to the limousine, Peggy turned to Holly and Ivy. "You two follow me." She pointed to a silver Audi. "That's my car over …"

"Peggy," a voice called.

Holly, Ivy and Peggy turned as a man coming out of the Country Club gave a slight wave.

"Oh," was all Peggy said as he started to walk over.

Holly thought she vaguely recognized the man. *Someone from the old neighborhood?* Blond, around 5'8", he had a sturdy look to him. He wore a tan three-piece suit with folded cuffs, no longer in style. Still it fit him well, but for some reason, she thought a suit was not this man's style. She could picture him in jeans and a tee-shirt. Definitely not the country club type.

"Who's that?" Ivy asked.

"Pat," Peggy said in a whisper, her eyes fixed on the man. "Patrick Keefe."

"Remember me?" he said, a shy smile lighting up his face.

"I — uh — of — of, course," Peggy stammered.

"I'm sorry about your mother, Peg," he said.

"Tha — thank you." Peggy opened her mouth, but no words came out. After a few moments she asked, "Were you here all the while — I mean inside for the service?"

"Yeah." Pat glanced down at his feet. When he looked up again, the shy smile returned. "I didn't want to bother you. Not with all those important people around you."

"Well, thank you — I'm — it's good to see you, Pat."

"Really good to see you, Peg."

Holly and Ivy watched as the pair just stared at one another.

"Hey, I remember you," Holly said. "You lived down the street from us in Kingsdale. I'm Holly Donnelly and this is my sister Ivy."

Pat broke into a wide grin. "Sure. You used to live at the top of the hill, right?"

"That's right!" Holly grinned. "Do you still live there?"

"Yep. I inherited the family house and been there ever since my wife passed away three years ago. How about you guys?"

"Well, we moved to New Jersey when we were kids. I still live there," Holly replied.

"And I live in South Carolina," Ivy added. "Sorry I don't remember you. I was only six years old when we moved."

"That was a long time ago." Pat laughed. "How long are you guys here for? Will you be passing through Kingsdale?"

"What do you say, Peggy? Will our treasure hunt take us to Kingsdale?" Holly turned to Peggy who appeared never to have taken her eyes off Pat. "Peggy?" Holly prompted when her cousin didn't reply.

Peggy blinked. "Oh, what was that?" she asked

"Will we be visiting Kingsdale?"

"Oh, um — I don't know..." Peggy replied.

"Well, if you do, please drop by," Pat said. "I'm home most days and if I'm not in the garden, I'm sitting on the front porch." He turned his gaze back to Peggy. "You know the house."

After a moment, Peggy nodded. "Uh-huh. Sure."

"Good to see you, Peg." Pat squeezed her forearm, and their eyes locked for a moment.

"Goo — good to see you too, Pat," she said.

Seeming reluctant to leave, he finally released his grip, turned and walked in the opposite direction of where Peggy was parked.

Holly slipped her arm around Peggy who started to sway, and whispered, "You want to tell us about you and Pat?"

Peggy swallowed hard and shook her head. "No. There's nothing to tell." She fumbled in her bag for her car fob. When she located them, she snapped her bag shut and said, "Just follow me."

As they watched Peggy get in her car, Ivy poked Holly. "We're going to Kingsdale, aren't we?"

Holly grinned. "What do you think?"

10 THE LOWE MANSION

Holly and Ivy took turns speculating about the relationship between Peggy and Patrick Keefe as they followed Peggy's Audi. After a few miles, they lapsed into silence. Once they were on the Luzerne-Dallas Highway, Ivy looked over at Holly. "Well, aren't you going to say anything about the treasure hunt?"

"What's there to say?" Holly grunted as she flipped on the turn signal and switched to the left lane behind Peggy's car.

"Oh, c'mon, Holly. This can be fun."

"Fun? This is going to be anything but fun. You know I didn't want to come here in the first place. I could be home working in my garden and spending the first weekend of summer break with my husband. But no. Now, not only are we stuck here the whole weekend, we have to stay in Aunt Peg's house. Aunt Peg for God's sake! I'm guessing she'll haunt each of us in our beds tonight. Why ..."

"Okay, okay. Stop," Ivy held up her hands in surrender. "Look, if nothing else, at least we'll help Jasmine pay off her college loans."

"Well, there is that," Holly admitted.

"I really like her." Ivy smiled.

"I like her, too."

"Twin nieces." Ivy stretched back in her seat. "I was so focused on seeing Fern again that I never thought about whether or not she had children. Whatever you think, I'm happy that this weekend will give us a chance to get to know them."

"Yeah, maybe. But there's something not right about this whole thing." Holly shook her head.

"What do you mean?"

"First of all, this is so *not* Aunt Peg. In my wildest dreams, I can't imagine her cooking up a whimsical idea like this treasure hunt, can you?"

"I barely remember her, so I honestly can't answer that."

"Well, trust me," Holly huffed. "Not her style. And what about Ron?"

"Georgette did say he's not taking his mother's death very well."

"Oh, pulleez!" Holly scoffed. "His behavior was absolutely boorish. He didn't even stop eating his salad during the opening prayer. And what about the way he jumped out of his seat before Peggy finished. He couldn't wait to get out of there."

"Not everyone grieves the same way." Ivy shrugged and looked out the side window. "Hey, do you have any ideas about the riddle?"

"When we get to Peggy's, the first thing I'll do is google Helios and Seshat. I think Helios is a sun god." Holly glanced over at Ivy. "What are you smiling about?"

"I just know you're going to be the one to figure out the answer to all the riddles."

"Oh, shut up."

****

Ivy peered through the windshield at the Tudor mansion as Holly pulled up and parked behind Peggy on the circular driveway. "Were you ever in this house?" she asked, her eyes wide with amazement.

"You mean this mansion," Holly replied. "No, I only heard about it. Our aunts used to talk about how Aunt Peg really married up when she landed Ronald Lowe, Jr."

"Clearly. So, I guess Ron is Ronald Lowe the Second and his son, Ronnie, is Ronald Lowe the Third."

"Yep. Ronnie didn't say very much, did he?" Holly said.

"No, but he seemed like a nice young man. He was attentive to his mother. If you ask me, they both seemed a little embarrassed by Ron's behavior."

As they got out of the car, Peggy came running over. Grinning wildly, she threw her arms around Holly. "I'm so happy you're here. I've been dreaming about this day for so long." She released Holly and hugged Ivy in turn. As Fern and her daughters got out of the limousine, she let go of Ivy and rushed over to greet them with the same effusive glee.

Ivy smiled. "She reminds me of a hummingbird."

"Yeah," Holly agreed. "I think she's way happier we're all here than we are."

Ivy frowned at her sister. "Speak for yourself," she said and headed over to the limousine. Holly let out a quiet sigh and followed.

"Come," Peggy said leading the way to the front entrance. "Let's go inside. I can't wait to show you around."

Peggy opened the front oak door more than twice her height and led the way into a grand entry hall. A huge round table, also oak, formed the centerpiece of the foyer. An assortment of potted plants was artistically arranged on the table to form a grand floral display.

"Oh, my!" Ivy said walking over to the table to examine the plants.

Violet joined her. "What a creative arrangement."

Peggy glowed. "I selected these specimens from the greenhouse especially for today."

"Wow!" Ivy exclaimed turning around. "You all see what she did here."

Holly approached the table. After a moment, she said, "Very clever, Peggy."

"What am I missing?" Jasmine asked.

"Look at the plants," her mother said, stepping nearer the display. Fern pointed to the plants as she named them. "Cinnamon Fern, Indian Jasmine, Blue Violet, Vining Ivy, and English Holly."

Peggy fluttered her hands, palms together, her signature silent applause. "I was so hoping you would notice."

A middle-aged man entered the foyer from a doorway at the back of the room. Dressed in a classic butler uniform, he walked over to Peggy.

"Everything ready, Higgins?" she asked.

"Yes, Miss," he replied crisply. "The luggage will be taken upstairs and Mrs. Higgins says drinks and snacks are ready on the patio whenever you are. Shall I escort the ladies to their rooms?"

"Yes," Peggy said, turning back to face her guests. "Higgins will show you to your rooms and when you're ready, come back down and we'll meet out on the patio, okay? It's straight through that doorway there," she pointed. "Oh, this is going to be so much fun," she said and dashed off, disappearing through the doorway Higgins had entered.

"This way, ladies." Higgins proceeded around the oak table to the grand staircase. Fern and Violet followed, then Ivy. Jasmine smiled as she took Holly by the arm, leaning close to her ear.

"Higgins? Seriously?" she whispered as they started up the stairs together.

This time Holly bit her lower lip to keep from laughing loudly. Maybe this was going to be fun after all.

11 SUNSET

Violet stood on the patio admiring the view. A rolling velvet green lawn stretched to a stand of trees about a football field's distance from the back of the house. Beyond lay the Pocono Mountains.

"What a view!" Ivy exclaimed as she and Holly walked through the French doors onto the brick patio.

Violet turned and greeted them with a smile. "It is breath-taking, isn't it?"

"I'll say," Holly nodded. "If this were my house, I think I'd spend most of my time out here."

"I can't wait to visit the greenhouse." Ivy pointed to the elegant glass structure situated on the left mid-way between the patio and the woods. Taking Violet by the arm, she said, "Come let's sit down. We had a chance to chat with Jasmine just a bit, but we'd love to know more about you, Violet."

"Well, in spite of the fact that we're twins, Jaz and I are quite different." Violet's face morphed into a humorous grimace as they sank into the oversized cushions of a wicker loveseat. "We both went to the University of Miami, but I majored in biology and Jaz majored in political science. After graduation, she went to law school, and I took a position as a Research Assistant with the University of Miami. I've been with them ever since."

"Sounds a little like Ivy and me," Holly said. "I was the English major and she became a registered nurse."

Violet's phone chirped and she glanced at the screen. "Excuse me. I have to take this," she said getting up. "It's my husband."

As she walked to the far end of the patio, Ivy glanced over at the table set across the patio in front of a trellis covered with an evergreen clematis vine. Crystal glasses sat beside covered pitchers of water and iced tea. Three platters were situated in the center of the table, their contents hidden by tented covers.

"Wonder what's on those platters," Ivy mused.

"You can't possibly be hungry after that luncheon." Holly said.

"Not right now, but ..."

"Here you are!" Peggy tweeted, stepping out onto the patio. She had changed into a baggy pair of tan pants and a brown, peasant-style blouse. Holly wondered why everything she wore looked at least one size too big for her small frame. The drab colors didn't do anything for her either.

"Well, what are you waiting for?" Peggy waved in the direction of the table. "I know we just ate, but in case you're feeling peckish, there's cookies, fruit and crudités here," Peggy said, lifting the tent covers. "Just help yourselves."

As Ivy got up and walked over to the table to peruse the snacks, Higgins arrived wheeling a cart laden with a gold ice bucket and bottles of assorted liquors and wines. Behind him, Jasmine appeared dressed in skinny jeans and a long sleeve t-shirt. After a glance across the patio to where her sister was still on the phone, she walked over and sat down beside Holly.

"Am I the only one who changed into play clothes?" she asked.

"I would have, but we didn't pack any," Holly replied. Lowering her voice, she looked at her watch and moved closer to Jasmine. In a low voice she said, "I thought we'd be on our way home right now."

After pouring Ivy an iced tea, Peggy turned around. "So, what would you two ladies like to drink?"

Jasmine got up and surveyed the table and liquor cart. "I don't mean to be ungracious, Aunt Peggy, but do you have any beer?"

Ivy burst out laughing. "Oh, my goodness. I'm beginning to see a distinct resemblance between you and your Aunt Holly."

Jasmine aimed an amused smile at Holly. "You're a beer drinker?"

Holly returned the smile and nodded.

"Sorry," Peggy shrugged. "I never expected any of you ladies to be beer drinkers. Higgins, could you bring out some beer?"

"Yes, Ma'am," he said. "Which do you prefer? Heineken, Stella Artois, Michelob Dry ..."

"Michelob Dry," Holly and Jasmine said simultaneously.

This time everyone laughed.

"Oh, isn't this fun already," Peggy said, releasing a sigh of contentment. After a moment, she turned to Jasmine. "You know, technically, I'm not really your aunt because I'm your mother's cousin, not her sister. I think that makes me your cousin once removed."

"Still, I wouldn't feel right calling you by your first name. Do you mind us calling you Aunt Peggy?" Jasmine asked.

"No." Peggy's eyes glistened as she placed her hand over her heart. "No, I actually love it."

Violet returned to the group, stuffing her phone in her

pocket. "I heard you all laughing over here," she said, dropping onto one of the cushioned armchairs. "What's so funny?"

"Let's just say Aunt Holly and I have a few things in common," Jasmine replied.

"Where's your mother?" Peggy asked.

"She said she needed to rest." Jasmine's tone conveyed her skepticism.

"Well, we were up quite early." Violet shot her sister an annoyed look.

"That's a little disappointing, but," Peggy gave her hand a dismissive wave "we certainly can get started solving the riddle and she can join us later."

"Darn," Holly said. "I meant to bring my laptop down to search Helios and Seshat."

"Oh, I can do that on my phone," Violet offered, pulling the iPhone back out of her pocket.

"Okay, search Helios first. I believe he's a sun god," Holly said.

Violet tapped in the letters. "Here." She looked up from the screen and smiled at Holly. "You're right. It says 'in Greek mythology, Helios is the sun god, sometimes called a Titan. He drove a chariot daily from east to west across the sky and sailed around the northerly stream of Ocean each night in a huge cup.'"

"Hey, I'm impressed." Jasmine patted Holly on the shoulder. "How did you know that?"

"Holly's an English professor," Ivy answered before Holly could.

"Oh, so there is a use for an English major," Jasmine teased.

Holly reduced her eyes to slits as she eyed her niece. "Just when I was starting to like you."

Amid the laughter that followed the exchange, Higgins appeared with two frosted mugs and a silver bowl filled with cans of Michelob Dry partially buried in ice.

Jasmine jumped up, "Just kidding, Aunt Holly. Let me get you a beer."

As Jasmine went over to the table, Ivy said, "Hey, let's get back to the riddle. I don't remember the exact words, but it definitely sounded something like what Violet just read."

"Where Helios ends his daily chariot ride you will find a gift from Seshat," Violet said.

Holly, Ivy and Peggy all stared at Violet for a moment.

"How did you do that — remember the quote word for word?" Ivy asked.

"Oh, Vy's got one of those oddball memories," Jasmine said as she returned to the circle, handing Holly a mug and a can of beer. "She can recite almost anything once she's heard it."

"Growing up it was a blessing and a curse." Violet frowned. "In some ways it was good, but I quickly became the person everyone ran to when they wanted to settle an argument about who said what. It always put me in the middle, and I hated it."

"But I'll bet you didn't have to take notes in class," Ivy said.

Violet chuckled. "Yeah, that was the upside."

"Okay, back to the riddle." Jasmine rolled her hand in a let's-get-going gesture. "Those college loans aren't going to pay themselves."

Holly snickered and took a sip of beer. "Okay, so where does Helios end his daily ride?

"In the West," Ivy replied.

"That certainly doesn't narrow things down," Violet frowned.

"Try googling Seshat." Holly suggested.

After a few keystrokes, Violet read, "Seshat, in ancient Egyptian religion, the goddess of writing and measurement and the ruler of books."

"Oh boy," Ivy shook her head. "So, we've got the West and writing and books. How does that help us?"

"Yeah, what are we looking for?" Jasmine asked. "Some Larry McMurtry cowboy novel?"

"Hold on." Violet remained focused on her phone. "It says here 'Mistress of the House of Books is another title for Seshat.'"

Holly sat forward, a spark in her eyes, "Well, a house of books is a library."

"Oh," Ivy smiled. "You think the location for the next clue might be in a library?"

"Could it be as simple as the library here in the house?" Jasmine asked.

"But what about the West?" Ivy turned to Peggy who hadn't said a word throughout the discussion. "Does the library here face the West?"

Peggy shook her head.

"So, Peggy aren't you going to help us at all?" Holly asked.

Peggy tilted her head just a tad, a contented smile on her face. "No. Sorry, I can't, but I can tell you, you're doing just great. Don't stop."

"Hmpf," Jasmine took a long swallow of beer. "Okay, let's think of other words for West."

"Wait a minute," Ivy's expression grew serious. "What happens at the end of Helios' ride?"

"The sun goes down," Violet replied.

"Sunset," a voice said from outside the circle.

Everyone turned to see Fern standing in the doorway. "Sunset was the name of the public beach at Hawzey Lake when we were kids."

12 RIDDLE NUMBER TWO

"Sunset?" Holly's expression slowly shifted from puzzlement to recognition as her memory kicked in. "That's it. I remember the beach at Sunset. We used to stop at the Grotto on our way home from the lake. Is that pizza place still there, Peggy?"

Peggy nodded as she jumped up and scurried over to where Fern remained standing in the doorway. Taking her by the arm, Peggy said, "Come. Let's get you a drink."

"So, Peggy," Holly continued as her cousin walked Fern over to the refreshment table, "are you going to at least tell us if we get the answer to the riddle right?"

"Yes, that only seems fair," Ivy added.

Peggy handed Fern a crystal glass. "Help yourself. There's wine, sparkling water, iced tea." She turned back to face Holly and Ivy. "Okay. I can tell you this much. You're half right."

"So, what are we supposed to do now?" Jasmine asked. "Go to this Sunset Beach and look for a library?"

Peggy smiled. "Bingo!"

"Okay, then." Holly finished what was left of her beer, got up and carried her mug and beer can over to the table. "Let's go."

"Right now?" Peggy looked gobsmacked.

Holly glanced at her watch. "Why not? It's just a little after two."

"We can go to Sunset first thing tomorrow. Don't you want to just talk and enjoy each other's ..." Peggy began.

"Holly's right," Fern cut in. "Sunset can't be more than a fifteen-minute drive from here." She put her glass down and headed back inside. "The sooner we solve these riddles, the sooner we can all go home. I'll be waiting out front."

Peggy appeared crestfallen. "All right. I'll go get my bag and have Higgins bring the mini-van around."

Violet got up and looped her arm through Peggy's. "Don't feel bad. Mom just gets cranky when she's tired."

"Yeah." Jasmine stood up and took Peggy by the other arm. "Besides, we'll have another riddle to solve when we get back. We can sit and talk about it all night long."

Peggy's expression brightened. "Yes. We can do that, can't we?"

As the twins walked Peggy towards the French doors, Jasmine looked back over her shoulder at Holly. Winking, she said, "Could you see that Higgins keeps those beers on ice."

"Gosh, I love these girls." Ivy poked Holly in the ribs. "I don't know about you, but I'm having a ball."

****

When Holly and Ivy got outside, Fern was already seated in the shotgun seat. Violet and Jasmine stood beside the open side door of a gleaming white Pontiac Transport mini-van.

"Didn't they stop making these vans?" Holly asked.

"Yeah," Jasmine nodded. "In 1999."

"But it looks brand new," Ivy said, admiring the scratch-free surface of the van.

Peggy suddenly appeared, her handbag slung over her shoulder and the car keys in hand. "That's because it only has 35,000 miles on it," she said as she got in the driver's seat.

"Come on, Aunt Ivy," Violet said. "I'll sit with you in the wayback."

"The wayback?" Ivy wrinkled her forehead.

"Yes, we had one of these when my kids were small. That's what we call the seat in the very back."

As they climbed in, Jasmine flashed Holly a sardonic grin. "And you're with me, Aunt Holly." She leaned in close and whispered, "You made sure about those beers, right?"

Holly smiled. "Yes. I instructed Higgins he might want to order more for the rest of our stay."

Jasmine let out a belly laugh. "Okay," she said as she followed Holly in and slid the door shut. "Sunset, here we come."

Before Peggy reached the end of the driveway, Jasmine started to sing. "Ninety-nine bottles of beer on the wall ..."

"Jasmine, shut up!" Fern said sternly without turning around.

Jasmine glanced at Holly, giving her eyes a slight roll. "Lighten up, Mom," Jasmine soothed. "I believe Aunt Peg would want us to have fun. I mean, anyone who would dream up this little escapade had to have a sense of humor, don't you think?"

This time Fern turned to face her daughter. "No, I don't. Your Great Aunt Peg had no sense of humor. She must have lost her mind at the end to come up with this crazy idea. Now, I'm here for one reason only — you girls. So, show me some respect and stop trying to turn this into some fun-filled campfire girls jamboree."

The only sound following Fern's outburst was the clicking of the turn signal as Peggy brought the car to a full stop at the end of the driveway. She glanced nervously over at Fern.

"Really, Fern, my mother …"

"I don't want to hear it," Fern said, staring out the passenger side window.

Jasmine exchanged a glance with Holly and let out a small sigh.

For the next few miles, they rode in complete silence until Ivy said, "Oh my goodness. Look there on the right, Holly. The Ranch Wagon."

"Considering all the bad press hot dogs get these days, I can't believe they're still in business," Holly said.

"Oh yes," Peggy said. "They've become quite a landmark."

"Foot-long hot dogs." Violet read the sign as they drove by. "Is that their specialty?"

"Yep." Ivy nodded. "I remember how delicious they were. Peggy, will we have a chance to stop and get some while we're here?"

"Well, I suppose I could send Higgins out to pick some up for lunch one day."

"Good old Higgins," Jasmine snickered.

The rest of the drive Holly, Ivy and Peggy exchanged comments about how certain things along the highway had changed and others hadn't. Fern didn't join in, but Holly noticed her posture soften a bit. She even turned to look at the Brookside Dairy where their parents used to bring them for ice cream.

"Wow!" Holly said as Peggy pulled up and parked the car in front of a row of houses. The lake was only partially visible through the space between houses. "This is so changed. I can't believe it."

As they piled out of the car, Fern asked, "What happened to the beach?"

Peggy sighed. "The owners sold it to a developer, and they

built these houses on it."

Holly peeked between two of the homes facing the lake. "Gosh, I remember when we'd drive past on our way to Sandy Bottom. There used to be a food stand right here."

"You could smell the French Fries as we drove past." Fern actually smiled.

"And the vinegar they used to sprinkle on them!" Holly added.

The sisters exchanged a brief glance at the memory. Fern was the first to look away.

"Hey, aren't we supposed to be looking for a library?" Jasmine asked.

Ivy looked down the road to where it bent around the lake. "Nothing but houses down that way."

"Same this way," Violet said surveying the road in the opposite direction. "Wait a minute." She put her hand over her forehead blocking out the sun. "What's that down there?"

"I don't see anything but houses," her sister replied.

"Look past the telephone pole." Violet started walking at a clip in the direction she pointed. She had a lead of several yards by the time the others began to follow.

As they neared the telephone pole, Ivy said, "Oh, I see what she's talking about."

"Oh my goodness! That's it!" Holly exclaimed picking up her pace. "A Little Free Library. I read about those."

When they reached the spot, Violet had already opened the door of what appeared to be a miniature red schoolhouse perched on a platform atop a two-by-four. She reached inside and retrieved an envelope. Breaking the seal, she pulled out a notecard.

"What's it say?" Holly asked.

"Congratulations on solving Riddle Number One. Good luck with Riddle Number Two." Violet paused for a moment, smiled, and continued. "Here goes: 'Where the noisy water roars and the eternal beating organ pulses, at the collier's gate, you'll find what you seek'."

13 MEMORY LANE

"Was Mrs. Higgins angry?" Ivy asked before she bit into her foot-long Ranch Wagon hot dog.

Peggy laughed. "No. As a matter of fact, she hadn't started to prepare dinner yet, so no harm done."

"Have Ranch Wagon hot dogs ever been served in this dining room before?" Holly asked, looking up at the gleaming crystal chandelier before she bit into her hot dog.

"No, pretty sure not," Peggy chuckled. "I think I'd remember that."

"Mmm." Jasmine closed her eyes savoring her first bite of the chili-dog she ordered.

"These are pretty good," Violet nodded, wiping a smear of mustard from her chin, "even if they really aren't very good for us."

"Enough about the hot dogs already," Fern snapped. "Let's get back to the riddle," she said, not looking at anyone in particular.

"Oh yeah," Holly nodded. "Violet, tell us again what it said."

Violet took a moment to chew and swallow, then recited, "Where the noisy water roars and the eternal beating organ pulses, at the collier's gate, you'll find what you seek."

"Sounds like there's more to figure out this time and nothing specific to google," Ivy said. "Where do we start?"

"At the beginning, of course." Holly lifted her newly frosted mug and took a swallow.

"So, what's noisy water?" Jasmine asked.

"A waterfall," Violet offered.

"Buttermilk Falls," Holly and Fern said at the same time, their eyes connecting briefly.

Fern turned to Peggy. "If that's right, I know Aunt Peg was not in her right mind. That was a major climb when we were kids. I certainly can't hike up there now."

Peggy frowned and let out a loud sigh. "Okay, I can tell you it's not Buttermilk Falls."

"Good." Fern added some relish to her hot dog.

"What else is noisy water?" Violet asked.

"A babbling brook," her sister suggested.

"Bear Creek?" Ivy said.

"Maybe." Holly squinted as she considered the possibility. "But where would someone hide a clue there? Let's move on to the next part of the riddle. What was it again, Violet?"

"'And the eternal beating organ pulses.'"

"Could it be a church organ?" Fern asked.

Ivy waved her hand. "I've got it. It's the heart. The heart is an organ that pulses non-stop."

"Very good, Aunt Ivy." Jasmine smiled in admiration. "Okay, so we've got a babbling brook and an eternal heart."

"What's a collier?" Violet asked.

"A coal miner," Holly and Fern said simultaneously. This time the sisters shared a brief smile.

"A babbling brook, an eternal heart and a coal miner." Jasmine pursed her lips and blew. "I certainly don't have any ideas. Looks like you three sisters are going to have to figure this out."

"I don't know." Ivy shook her head, but after a moment, moved to the edge of her chair. "Hey, didn't the lawyer refer to this whole thing as a trip down memory lane?"

"Yeah," Holly said. "That's right."

"Then, for sure, only you three can figure this out," Violet said looking in turn at Holly, Ivy and her mother.

"So think," Jasmine commanded. "Sunset was a place you all used to go to when you were kids. What's a place with a babbling brook, an eternal heart and a coal mine?"

"If Aunt Peg didn't intend for us to hike up to Buttermilk Falls, she surely didn't intend for us to visit a coal mine," Ivy said.

"Besides, all the coal mines are closed," Fern added. "Have been for years."

"Wait a minute," Holly said, the spark of recognition in her eyes. "Nay Aug Park had a coal mine."

"Oh my goodness!" Ivy exclaimed. "We went there every Memorial Day. I remember that coal mine. It used to scare me to go in there."

"Violet, can you google Nay Aug Park in Scranton on your phone?"

"Sure." Violet pulled out her phone and tapped in the letters. "Here it is. Oh, this looks so nice."

Jasmine leaned over to view the screen as Violet scrolled through the photos. "Stop, stop, stop," she said, "Go back. There!" she pointed to a spot on the screen. The twins grinned, looked up and together said, "Brooks Mine."

Violet continued to scroll. "There are pictures of waterfalls and what I'd call 'babbling brooks.'"

"But what's the heart got to do with it?" Ivy asked.

Holly snapped her fingers. "What's the name of the museum?"

Violet scrolled some more. She and Jasmine shared an even wider grin as they both said, "Everhart."

Ivy laughed, "Eternal beating organ!"

"Oh, this has to be it," Violet said. "Listen to this. The name Nay Aug traces its origin to the Munsee Indians, a sub-group of the larger Lenape tribe. In their language Nay Aug means "noisy water or roaring brook.'"

Wearing a gleeful smile, Peggy fluttered her hands in silent applause. "I knew you girls could do it."

"So tomorrow we drive to Scranton?" Ivy asked.

"Yes, we do. We'll leave at 10:00 sharp," Peggy replied. "Mr. and Mrs. Higgins are leaving at noon for an overnight visit to her sister's in Port Jervis. Before they leave Mrs. Higgins will prepare a picnic for us to take. We can eat at the park. It'll be just like old times."

"So you were pretty sure we'd figure this out." Fern gave Peggy a penetrating stare.

Peggy's expression turned serious. "Yes, Fern. I was counting on your memories — Holly's and Ivy's — that they would be as powerful as mine. We did have a wonderful childhood, didn't we?"

Before Fern could respond, the sound of a door slamming caught everyone by surprise. Peggy appeared alarmed as she turned to the arched doorway that led out into the hall. She stood up, but sank down again as Ron's bulky frame filled the archway.

Wild-eyed, he scanned the room. "What the hell is going on here?"

14 CURIOUSER AND CURIOUSER

"Well, Peggy?" Ron glared at his stepsister who sat frozen in her chair. "Mom hated these ..."

"Stop!" Peggy shouted jumping to her feet. "What — what are you doing here?"

"I came here because that gasbag Hiram Thurston called me again and ..."

"Not here, Ron." Don appeared in the doorway behind his brother.

Peggy rushed over to where Don stood. "What's ..."

"Let's go in the office." Don met his brother's scowl with a calm, but resolute expression. "Come on, Ron," he said as he put an arm around Peggy.

Ron took one last look around the table. "All of you, get out of my mother's house." He turned and stormed out of the room.

A tearful Peggy turned to the group. "Don't listen to him. This is my house and you're my guests."

"Come, Peggy." Don gently guided her out of the room.

Holly, Ivy, Fern and the twins sat silently staring at the now vacant doorway.

"What a guy!" Jasmine said, leaning back in her chair.

"Maybe we should go," Ivy said. "We don't want to cause any problems for Peggy."

Fern stood up, a stony expression on her face. "Ron is nothing but a petty tyrant. I'll not be bullied by him. I'm going to bed."

After she left the room, Violet shook her head. "What do you think is going on here?"

"I have no idea." Holly shook her head. Stifling a yawn, she looked at her watch. "Oh, brother, I need to call Nick. I texted him earlier and said we wouldn't be home tonight and that I'd call and explain later." She got up. "It's now way later."

Ivy got up. "I'm feeling tired, too. See you girls in the morning."

Jasmine looked at Violet. "I'm with them. Let's go."

"Mom certainly had a low opinion of Ron," Violet said as she got up. "What do you think that's all about?"

"I don't know, but this visit is getting curiouser and curiouser." Jasmine headed to the doorway.

"Hey, shouldn't we at least take the dishes to the kitchen?" Violet scanned the table.

"What? And put the Higginses out of work? Besides, I want to be locked safely in my room before the return of Raging Ron."

Violet nodded. "Good idea."

****

"So what do you think?" Ivy asked after Holly closed and locked their bedroom door.

"I think Ron doesn't know anything about this treasure hunt, making me highly suspicious of this 'unique provision' of the will," Holly replied, dropping onto her bed.

"Suspicious how?"

"Look, he's an heir. He had to have been given a copy of the will. That's the law."

"We didn't get a copy of the will," Ivy said.

"Exactly," Holly replied.

Ivy stared at her sister and after a moment smiled. "You think this treasure hunt is Peggy's idea."

"Bingo!"

"So, she's giving us *her* money? Why in the world would she do that?"

"Good question." Holly shook her head as she rooted around in her handbag trying to locate her phone.

"What do you think the thing with Hiram is all about?"

"Another good question that I don't have the answer to." Holly pulled her phone out of her handbag and paused, "Remember after the memorial service when Hiram was talking to us? The woman who greeted us at the door came over and whispered something to him. He looked concerned, made an excuse and left pretty abruptly."

"You think that's what Ron and Don coming here is all about?" Ivy asked.

"Yes. He said Hiram called him again," Holly replied. "But you know what? None of that is our business. The good news is we solved two riddles today. At this rate, we can probably wrap things up tomorrow afternoon and be on our way back home for dinner."

"Ya think?" Ivy appeared uncertain.

"Honestly? No." Holly said. "Now go use the bathroom and let me call Nick."

Ivy grabbed her toiletries bag. As she closed the bathroom door, Holly tapped in the phone number.

"Hi, honey. Sorry for the delay, but the good news is we should be back tomorrow this time," she said, her fingers crossed.

15 NAY AUG PARK

"Like hell, you will!" a man's voice shouted.

Holly and Ivy stopped at the top of the grand staircase and watched as Hiram Thurston rushed past, Ron right behind him. "Do this and you'll regret it," Ron shouted following Hiram out the front door. As the door slammed shut, the shouting continued, but the sisters could no longer make out what Ron was saying.

"Maybe we should go back to our room and wait for Peggy to come and get us," Ivy whispered.

Just then, Don and Peggy came into view. His head downcast, Don paused. He put his hand on Peggy's shoulder. "This is not good, Peggy."

"Ahem." Holly cleared her throat.

Peggy and Don both looked upward as Holly and Ivy started down the stairs.

"I'll try to talk to him before Georgette and I leave this afternoon," Don said.

"Oh, you don't need to worry about him," Peggy said. "You and Georgette just go and have a great time."

Don gave his stepsister's shoulder a squeeze and kissed her on the cheek. He turned to face Holly and Ivy as they reached the bottom of the staircase. "Enjoy the rest of your stay," he said, then turned and left through the front door.

"Don and Georgette going away?" Ivy asked.

Peggy forced a smile. "Yes, they booked a four-day cruise to Bar Harbor months ago. It leaves out of Boston. They fly there this afternoon."

"How nice," Ivy said. "You and Nick should do something like that, Holly."

"Yes," her sister agreed. "That would be nice." Turning to Peggy, she said, "We couldn't help hearing Ron shouting. Everything all right?"

"Yes." Peggy sighed. "Our brother Ron is just a bit of a hothead. Not your concern." She waved her hand, her smile more genuine this time. "Did you enjoy breakfast?"

"Oh yes," Ivy said. "Breakfast in our room was quite a treat."

"Good morning, Aunties," Jasmine said from the top of the stairs. She rubbed her hand on the banister. "I'd love to slide down this thing."

"Jasmine!" Fern said, her tone sharp.

"Just kidding, Mom." Jasmine scoffed as she adopted the posture of a runway model and did a catwalk down the steps, her mother and Violet behind her.

"Was that Ron shouting?" Fern asked. "Didn't he go home last night?"

"Yes, but we had an early morning meeting," Peggy replied. "It's over now." She headed to the door. "Higgins brought the van around packed with our picnic lunch, so let's get going."

Outside, there was no sign of Ron or Hiram. Everyone assumed the same seats they had on the drive to Sunset the day before.

"I'm really looking forward to this," Ivy said.

"Me too," replied Violet.

"Yeah, she practically read me the entire Nay Aug Park website when we went upstairs last night," Jasmine crossed her eyes.

As they drove, Violet filled them in on details of interest concerning the park and the current exhibition at the museum.

"Well, here we are," Peggy said as she drove past the Nay Aug Park sign.

Once everyone was out of the van, Jasmine said, "Shall we go straight to the mine?"

"If that's what you want," Peggy said. "It's this way." She led them to a footpath.

After a brisk five-minute walk, Ivy pointed to a stone archway visible in the distance. "There it is."

As they drew nearer, Holly grimaced. "It looks like the gate is locked."

"Yes," Peggy said. "You can no longer go inside."

"What's in there?" Jasmine asked.

"It's an actual model coal mine. The walls are all anthracite," Peggy replied.

"I remember there were little rooms carved into the walls that had exhibits of coal miners at work," Ivy said. "But if we can't get inside, how will we find the next clue?"

Fern turned to Violet. "Remind us how the riddle goes."

"Where the noisy water roars and the eternal beating organ pulses, at the collier's gate, you'll find what you seek."

"Then, let's go check out the gate." Holly said.

When they reached the mine entrance, they each began examining every section of the ten-foot-tall gate—pickets, the lock, even the hinges.

"I don't see anything." Fern frowned.

"If there was an envelope like the last time, it might have blown inside," Ivy said, peering through the gate pickets, "but I don't see anything."

"Hold on." Jasmine walked over to a small boulder on the right side of the gate. "Vy, help me."

Together the twins rolled the boulder over. As Violet brushed away leaves, Jasmine snatched a soiled envelope and jumped up. "We got it." She raised her arms over her head and did a small victory dance.

"Quit clowning," Fern snapped. "Just open the envelope and read it."

Jasmine tore open the envelope. "Behind where Hestia reigns, and Demeter rules, a place you know well, the treasure you hunt awaits you. Bonus Clue 1. Rocks and stones don't hurt my bones. Bonus Clue 2. Carton + the boy on the raft will help you name me."

16 JUST LIKE OLD TIMES

"White meat or dark?" Peggy asked as she pulled two plastic containers of fried chicken out of the small cooler Mrs. Higgins prepared.

"Dark for me," Holly said reaching for the container with legs and thighs.

Jasmine and Violet helped pass the napkins, paper plates and plastic cutlery. Ivy opened an insulated cooler bag and passed around the drinks. After they filled their plates and began to eat, the conversation focused on the quality of Mrs. Higgins' fried chicken and potato salad.

"Okay," Fern intervened. "Enough of the chit chat. Any suggestions about this riddle?"

"There's so much packed into this one." Holly sighed. "Violet, can you repeat it for us?"

"Allow me," Jasmine said, pulling the paper she and Violet had retrieved from under the boulder.

When she finished reading the riddle, Ivy sighed. "I guess we start where we did the last time--at the beginning. Who are Hestia and Demeter?"

Jasmine looked at Holly. "Well, Teach, what do you say?"

"I don't know Hestia, but Demeter is a goddess of the

garden," Holly replied. "Can you look Hestia up on your phone, Violet?"

Violet pulled her iPhone out of her pocket. "I don't have any bars. I can't connect to the internet."

Holly pulled out her phone. "Me either," she said. "Anyone else want to try?"

Jasmine shook her head. "I left my cell in my bedroom. I figured any calls from work could wait until we got back."

"Don't look at me." Ivy shrugged. "I still have a flip phone."

"No way!" Jasmine widened her eyes in disbelief as everyone laughed.

"I don't see what's so funny," Fern said. "I don't even have a cellphone. They're just a nuisance."

"Okay, so let's keep working the riddle. We can look Hestia up when we get home," Holly said. "My first guess is this treasure is in a garden, but we need to know who Hestia is to figure out where this garden is."

"So, what can't be broken by rocks and stones?" Violet asked.

Jasmine's eyes opened wide. "Diamonds!"

Fern shook her head. "I think it's highly unlikely Aunt Peg left us diamonds."

"I have to agree," Holly said.

"The last bonus clue really is the most confusing of all," Ivy shook her head. "Carton and the boy on the raft. What could that be?"

Holly shook her head. "I'm stumped."

Peggy stood up and started to pack up the unfinished food. "Well, why don't we drive home, and you can spend the rest of the afternoon working on this?"

"Aunt Ivy and I would like to visit the museum," Violet

said as she got up. "Maybe I can get something for my kids at the gift shop."

Holly laughed. "Oh, my sister doesn't want to visit the museum. She just can't pass up a visit to a gift shop."

"Ignore her," Ivy said as she looped her arm through Violet's and headed down the footpath to the museum.

Peggy smiled like a kid on Christmas morning. "Why don't you all go on and I'll pack up. I'll meet you there after I get this all in the car."

As Fern and Jasmine got up, Holly said, "I'll stay and help you."

"No, no," Peggy shook her head, still smiling. "You all go together. I'll be done here and join you in no time."

Holly gave Peggy an appraising look. "Just like old times, huh, Peggy?"

Peggy nodded, a dreamy look on her face as she watched the others walk down the path towards the museum. "Just like old times."

17 LET'S TALK

Holly was the first one to arrive at the patio after they returned from Nay Aug Park. She dropped down on one of the cushioned wicker chairs and started to text Nick. When she heard footsteps, she looked up as Fern appeared in the doorway. Fern stopped when she spotted Holly, then backed up a step as if to leave.

Holly jumped to her feet. "Fern, wait. Don't go. Come sit."

Fern remained standing in the doorway, poised to bolt.

"Please," Holly said. "We haven't had any time alone since this weekend started. Let's talk."

Fern took a deep breath and after a moment stepped onto the patio. She took a seat opposite Holly.

"Ivy and I are really enjoying getting to know the twins," Holly said.

Just the trace of a sour smile graced Fern's lips. When she didn't reply, Holly wondered if anything could break through her sister's hard shell. After a moment, she continued. "They're really wonderful young women."

Fern just nodded.

Holly sighed. "You're not making this easy, are you?"

"Why should I?" Fern's expression turned fierce. "I was disowned by all of you when I was just 17 years old. After all these years, you now want me to forget that, make nice and act like we're one, big, happy family?"

Tears stung Holly's eyes. "Look, I know you left home under a dark cloud, Fern, but Ivy and I had nothing to do with that. For God's sake, we were only six and nine years old. All we knew is one day we had a big sister and the next day she was gone. Nobody told us anything and when we asked Mom, she forbade us to talk about you. Our aunts weren't allowed to talk to us about you either. No matter how much I asked and begged, they wouldn't tell me anything." Holly brushed away a tear.

"What about those letters you sent?" Fern asked, her expression still hard and unyielding. "How did you always manage to find out where I was living? Somebody had to tell you something."

"The first time I found an address for you was at Aunt Peg's house in Kingsdale. Little Peggy invited us in for a soda, and I saw a stack of letters to be mailed on the counter. The top one was addressed to Fern Brennan. I knew it had to be you, so I copied the address down on a napkin and wrote you." Holly twisted her lips to the side. "Boy, did I get in trouble when that letter got returned. We weren't allowed in Aunt Peg's house after that."

"Then how did you get the address we moved to?" Fern asked.

"Little Peggy." Holly smiled. "She sort of looked up to me back then, so I would let her hang out with me in exchange for any information she could give me about you."

"I knew Aunt Peg wouldn't give it to you," Fern smirked and looked out past the patio to the greenhouse. Returning her gaze to Holly, she said, "You know, Aunt Peg was the only one who helped Tommy and me. She gave us money to take the bus to Florida. Her cousin Bridget lived there. We stayed with her for a while until we got our own place."

"When you left, were you …" Holly hesitated.

Fern glared at Holly. "Was I pregnant? No, I wasn't. We didn't even have sex until we got married in Florida."

"But weren't you too young to get married?"

"Bridget said she was my mother and gave her consent. I don't know how Aunt Peg got the documents we needed, but she did." Again, Fern's face grew fierce. "It was hard the first few years, but Tommy and me — we made it work. He was a good husband and a good father."

"He's passed?"

This time Fern's eyes got misty. "He had a heart attack right after the girls graduated from high school. Died instantly."

"I'm sorry," Holly said. "I remember Tommy. I liked him. I never understood what Mom had against him."

"Oh, he wasn't good enough, she said. She wanted her daughters to marry doctors and lawyers." Fern shook her head in disgust. "Don't know where I was supposed to meet one. There weren't many of those in Kingsdale, I'll tell you."

Holly got up and moved to the chair closer to Fern. "I'm sorry for everything that happened to you. But Ivy and I had nothing to do with it. Can we …"

Suddenly, Jasmine appeared in the doorway, her expression uncharacteristically grim. "You need to come with me."

When Fern and Holly remained seated, staring at her, Jasmine widened her eyes and said, "Now." Without waiting, she pivoted and disappeared back inside the house.

"Guess we better go," Holly said getting up.

Fern stood and together they followed in Jasmine's wake. She stopped outside the library where an ashen-faced Ivy and a tearful Violet were standing.

Fern grasped Violet's arm. "What's wrong?"

Violet threw her arms around her mother's neck and burst into tears.

Holly looked at Ivy. "What happened?"

Ivy started to say something, but no words came out of her mouth. Holly turned to Jasmine who scratched the back of her neck as she said, "There's a body in the library."

18 FINDING JASMINE

"Are you going to call Nick?" Ivy whispered.

"No!" Holly gave her head a vehement shake. She looked over to where Fern and Violet sat trying to comfort a tearful Peggy. "Not yet anyway," she sighed.

"Yeah. Best to wait." Ivy nodded. "I was really impressed with how Jasmine took charge. She knew exactly what to do and how to talk to the police."

Holly's mouth formed a wry smile. "Yes, it pays to have a lawyer in the family."

Ivy smiled, but her expression swiftly morphed into a pitiful grimace. "Oh, Holly. I'm so sorry."

"Why are you sorry?"

"I know you didn't want to come here."

Holly frowned. "I'll dispense with the told-ya-so's — for now. Come on. Let's go see if we can help out with Peggy."

Before they reached the wicker couch, a middle-aged man dressed in khaki pants and a plaid sport jacket stepped onto the patio. Holly thought he bore a resemblance to William Bendix, an older actor from a black and white television show she couldn't recall the name of. He had a broad face with full cheeks that made him appear chubbier than he actually was.

"Ladies," he said, "I'm Detective Jaworski with the Luzerne County Investigative Unit. Which one of you is Peggy Lowe?"

Peggy straightened up and dabbed at her eyes with a tissue. "I am."

The detective gave a slight nod. "Is there somewhere we could talk privately?"

Peggy quickly rose and started toward the door. "Yes, of course …"

"Peggy." Holly just as quickly moved in the same direction. "Let me get Jasmine."

"Who are you?" Jaworski asked.

"I'm Holly Donnelly, Peggy's cousin."

The detective squinted as he gave her an appraising once-over. "Ms. Donnelly, I'll talk to you and this Jasmine a little later."

Holly tilted her head and let out an audible sigh. "'*This Jasmine* is Ms. Lowe's attorney, Detective."

Jaworski shrugged dismissively. "No need. I just have a few questions for Ms. Lowe." He took Peggy by the arm and led her inside.

Holly's attempt to follow was blocked by a uniformed policeman who seemed to appear out of nowhere.

"You'll need to stay out here, Ma'am," the young officer said. Holly hesitated a moment, then pivoted and returned to the seating area. Without sitting down, her back to the door, she asked, "Is the policeman still there?"

Without moving her head, Fern's eyes darted to the doorway. "Uh-huh," she muttered softly.

"Let me know if he leaves," Holly said.

"What are you going to do?" Ivy asked, a worried expression clouding her face.

"I'm going to go find Jasmine. Peggy shouldn't talk to the

police without a lawyer."

"But surely she hasn't got anything to hide," Violet said.

"He's gone." Fern had not taken her eyes off the doorway until that moment.

"Great." Holly turned to go.

Ivy grasped her forearm. "Do you want me to go with you?"

"No. Just stand in the spot where I was standing in front of Violet and Fern. If the policeman glances out, he won't even notice I'm missing."

Ivy released her sister's arm and moved to the spot Holly indicated. She, Violet and Fern watched as Holly disappeared around the side of the mansion.

"Is she always like this?" Violet asked.

"No," Ivy replied. "Sometimes she's much worse."

****

Holly bent low as she passed the kitchen windows. She sneaked a peek, relieved to find no one inside. As she looked down the side of the house, she guessed the next set of windows belonged to the office and the ones after that would be the library—her target. Jasmine was likely still there observing as the forensic team did their work. She just needed to get her niece's attention for a moment.

A vehicle arriving in the drive caused Holly to duck behind the foundation shrubs. Looking ahead, she determined there was enough room between the shrubs and the house for her to remain hidden as she crept forward.

Again, she remained low as she approached the office windows. Slowly, she rose up to peek inside and spotted Jasmine through the open door, standing out in the hall talking to a policeman. She waved, but to no avail. Jasmine was standing at an angle facing away from the door.

Holly wondered if it was worth the risk of knocking on the glass. What did she have to lose? All that mattered was that she get Jasmine's attention. Just as her hand was poised to knock, Jasmine moved out of sight.

Holly crouched down and continued towards the library windows. When she reached her destination, she found the ground beneath the windows to be slightly lower than the ground beneath the office windows. She had to stand on her toes to see inside. She smiled when she saw that Jasmine was inside the room and facing the window. Making a fist she knocked so hard on the glass her knuckles hurt. No matter. Jasmine spotted her.

"Ma'am." A voice from behind startled Holly and she lost her footing falling backward on top of an azalea bush. When she looked up, she faced the policeman who'd told her she had to stay on the patio. As he reached for her to help get her back on her feet, the library window opened.

Jasmine leaned out and flashed Holly a puckish smile. "What are you doing?"

"A detective is questioning Peggy and this guy ..." Holly glared at the police officer, pulling her arm loose from his grip, "... wouldn't let me in the house to tell you. *That's* what I'm doing," she replied as she brushed leaves off her clothes.

Jasmine held her cell phone out the window in her left hand and pointed to it with her right index finger. "You have heard of texting, haven't you?"

19 SORRY

In the drawing room, Jasmine sat across from Jaworski, Holly beside her. "That won't be necessary, Detective." She stood up, looking down at her aunt. "Ms. Donnelly understands that what she did could be construed as interfering in a police investigation. She will obey police instructions without exception." Her left eyebrow arced upward. "Right, Aunt Holly?"

Holly bit her lip, glaring at her niece. When she didn't reply, Jasmine repeated in a more emphatic tone, "Right, Aunt Holly?"

"Right." Holly nodded and got up. "Am I free to go?" She turned her glare on the detective.

Jaworski glowered back. "For now."

"You know ..." Holly began.

"Aunt Holly," Jasmine took her by the arm, "you're free to go." She gave her aunt's arm a tug and led her to the door. When they both stepped out into the main hall, she closed the drawing room pocket doors behind them.

"He's insufferable," Holly scowled.

Jasmine gave her aunt's back a soothing pat. "Yes, but he's the law and I'm trying very hard to get through these interviews without anyone getting taken to the Luzerne County Jail."

Holly let out a heavy sigh. "I know that. You're doing a great job. I'm sorry."

"It's okay." Jasmine smiled.

The sound of footsteps drew their attention across the main hall to where Violet approached, escorted by the police officer who discovered Holly outside in the bushes.

"The officer will escort you back to the patio," Jasmine said as she slid the doors open and motioned for Violet to go inside.

Holly bared her teeth. "Oh, the indignity of it all," she muttered under her breath.

****

Only Ivy and Fern were on the patio when Holly returned.

"How'd it go?" Ivy asked.

"All right," Holly said, dropping down and nestling into one of the cushioned wicker chairs. "Where's Peggy?"

"That lawyer, Charles, just got here," Fern replied. "She went inside with him."

"What a mess," Ivy moaned. "How could this happen?"

Holly shook her head. "Good question."

"Well," Fern glanced from one sister to the other. "Jaworski left the room when I was in there and Jasmine told me it looks as if the victim was murdered elsewhere, and the body brought here."

"What?" Ivy's eyes widened in disbelief. "Why in the world would someone do that?"

"Well, if whoever murdered him did it in their own home, they sure as hell couldn't leave his body there," Holly said.

"It was Hiram Thurston, wasn't it?" Ivy asked.

Fern wrinkled her forehead. "Who's he?"

"The President of the Hawzey Lake Country Club." Holly

sat forward. "That's right. You weren't at the memorial service, and you didn't see him fly out of here yesterday morning having a shouting match with Ron."

"Ron. Of course." Fern sank back in her chair. "I remember hearing the shouting. When I asked what it was about, Peggy brushed it off. What were they arguing about?"

"Another good question." Holly got up and went over to the refreshment table. She opened the cooler and peered inside. "All I remember is Ron saying Hiram would regret whatever it was he was planning to do. Anyone want water?"

"Yeah," Ivy said. "Bring me a bottle, please."

"Me too," Fern nodded.

Ivy reached for the bottle Holly handed her. "You told the detective about the argument?" she asked.

"Yes, and when it's your turn, you should too." Holly handed a water bottle to Fern and returned to her chair.

"Do you think that's what Peggy would want us to do?" Ivy asked.

Fern unscrewed the bottle cap. "No. She'd want us to defend that snake." She raised the bottle to her lips and took a swallow.

"You really don't like him, do you?" Holly asked. "There some history there?"

"Yes." Fern raised her chin. "But I don't want to discuss history. Right now, I just want to get this inheritance for my daughters and get the hell out of here."

Holly raised her water bottle. "Well, there's something we can all agree on."

"Do you think Peggy would call off the treasure hunt and just let us go home?" Ivy asked.

Holly slowly turned her head from side to side. "It may not

be up to her. The police might not let us leave. Besides, Peggy seems so hell bent on all of us being here together, I doubt she'd call off the treasure hunt."

Fern took a deep breath and looked first at Ivy, then at Holly. "You're right. And maybe Peggy's been right too." She took another sip of water. "This weekend has … well, let's just say I thought about what you said before, Holly. I've been harboring a lot of hard feelings towards the family for so many years." She paused, looking down at the water bottle. "You two were just kids when I left and — well, let's just say, I may have transferred my feelings towards Mom onto you without thinking, and that was — that was unfair to you. I'm sorry."

Holly's eyes glistened as she watched Ivy walk over and hug Fern. "I think this is what Peggy was hoping for."

Fern dabbed her eyes with a tissue. After a moment she said, "Okay, enough of this." Her expression became more determined. "It can't take the police too long to figure out that we had nothing to do with this murder. Jasmine will see to that. In the meantime, we've done pretty well solving the riddles so far. Do you think we can work together to solve the last riddle? Then we can all go home."

"Absolutely," Ivy said.

Holly filled her cheeks with air and blew it out slowly. "We can do that for sure. But can we really just collect our money, pack up and leave Peggy alone to deal with this murder? How can we desert her now?"

20 PHONE CALLS

Holly stretched out on the bed and punched in Nick's cell number.

"Hi, Honey," she said in as cheerful a voice as she could muster.

"You on your way home?" Nick asked.

"Well, that's why I'm calling. I've got good news and bad news."

"Uh-oh. Do I have to …"

"No, no. Relax." Holly bit her lip. "Let me start with the good news. The good news is we've solved the first two riddles and we're working on the third. We should have it worked out before we go to bed."

"And I guess the bad news is you're not coming home to-night," Nick said.

"Yeah. Unfortunately, we need another day."

"No problem," Nick soothed. "I suppose Lucky and me can muddle through another night without you."

Holly let out a soft laugh. "I miss you."

"Miss you, too. Things going okay with Fern?" Nick asked.

"Yes, I think we had a real breakthrough today." Holly told

THE BLOOMING TREASURE MURDER

Nick about Fern's apology.

"That's great. Nothing more important than family," Nick said. "Ivy must be happy."

"Yeah. Me too." Holly glanced at her watch.

"Oh, I almost forgot. Kate called. I told her about the memorial service."

"Okay, I'll give her a call," Holly said. "Listen, I better get going. They said dinner would be ready soon when I came upstairs to make this call."

"Okay. So, I'll see you tomorrow."

Holly crossed her fingers, glad Nick could not see her grimace. "Yes. See you tomorrow. Love you."

"*Ti amo, mi amore.*"

As soon as Nick's number disappeared from the screen, Holly noticed she'd missed a text message. She tapped the icon and saw it was from Kate.

"*My grandmother visited in a dream last night. Think the message was for you. Call me.*"

Holly sighed. This couldn't be good. Her friend Kate's grandmother, who died years before Holly even met Kate, always seemed to turn up with a message whenever a dead body popped up. The problem was the messages were never very clear, though the one she got in Tuscany did save Nick's life.

Holly tapped the call icon. "Hi, Kate. Just noticed your message. What's up?"

"Okay, so what have you been up to? Nona was quite agitated in last night's dream."

"What did she say?"

"The hummingbird is in danger," Kate replied.

Holly caught her breath remembering Ivy saying Peggy reminded her of a hummingbird. "What makes you think that was a message for me?"

"Because she followed that up with 'Tell the teacher'."

"Oh no," Holly groaned.

"So are you going to tell me what's going on?" Kate asked.

"Okay, so here's what's happened since we got here." Holly recounted as succinctly as possible the events that occurred since their arrival on Friday evening.

"Well, it looks like Nona finally sent you a very clear message," Kate said when she finished. I take it your cousin Peggy is the hummingbird."

"Yes," Holly replied. "And you know what this means?"

"What?"

"It means, once again, like it or not, we're involved in a murder investigation and we can't leave here until this murder is solved."

21 HESTIA AND DEMETER

The kitchen was a beehive of activity when Holly arrived. Fern was laying out placemats and napkins that matched the island's granite countertop. Violet followed with plates and Ivy with the silverware. Jasmine was filling a pitcher from the refrigerator water dispenser.

Holly looked across the kitchen to where Peggy leaned against the counter, watching it all, smiling. Definitely not in hummingbird mode at the moment. What kind of danger was she in? Holly walked over to join her and asked, "How are you doing?"

"I'm okay." Peggy managed only a weak smile.

"I'm sorry about Hiram. He seemed to be a good friend of your family."

"Yes." Peggy nodded. "He was. After my stepfather died, Mother relied on him for advice, and he was always there for her."

"Have you been able to reach the Higginses?"

Peggy shook her head. "Detective Jaworski took Mrs. Higgins' sister's number. He said for me to let the police contact them."

"Peggy, you know we heard Ron threaten ..."

"Excuse me. I think that was the doorbell. The food must be here." Peggy rushed off leaving Holly's sentence unfinished.

Jasmine who'd been lingering at the refrigerator, listening, walked over to Holly. "She won't even consider the possibility that Ron had anything to do with it."

"What about the police?" Holly asked.

"Jaworski was headed over to Ron's as soon as he finished up here."

"Do you think they'll arrest him?"

Jasmine frowned. "Not yet. They have to process the evidence first. For now, they'll just question him."

"What are you two conspiring about?" Ivy asked as she laid the last fork next to a plate.

"We're just trying to decide whether or not we need to make a beer run before Higgins returns tomorrow," Jasmine said.

"Uh-huh." Ivy waggled her head. "Like I believe that."

"Food's here." Peggy said as she entered the kitchen and held up two bags of take-out.

Violet reached for the bags. "Let me take those. We've got the serving bowls ready."

Ivy immediately joined her and started opening the containers.

"Jasmine, come fill those water glasses," Fern commanded.

"Yes, mother," Jasmine said in her most saccharine voice.

Fern ignored the sarcasm and motioned Holly over. "C'mon. Help get this food on the table so we can start working on the riddle."

"Oh, right. The riddle." Holly walked over to the counter, relieved they had something besides the body in the library to focus on. She grabbed a bowl of pasta salad and a bread tray. As she took her seat at the island, she said, "Okay, Violet. Do your thing."

As everyone took their places, Violet began her recitation. "Behind where Hestia reigns, and Demeter rules, a place you know well, the treasure you hunt awaits you. Bonus Clue 1. Rocks and stones don't hurt my bones. Bonus Clue 2. Carton + the boy on the raft will help you name me."

"I looked up Hestia before I called Nick. I didn't remember her." Holly took a roll from the bread plate and passed it to Fern. "She's the Greek goddess of the family hearth."

"And Demeter?" Ivy asked, spooning pasta salad on her dish.

"Oh, I know that one," Violet smiled. "She's the goddess of agriculture."

Jasmine's forehead wrinkled as she stared at her sister. "How did you know that?"

"Lilly's class had to do a report on Greek gods and goddesses," Violet replied. "She picked Demeter."

"Your daughter's name is Lilly?" Ivy chuckled. "Continuing the tradition of flowery names for Donnelly women, I see."

"And she named her son, Reed," Jasmine scoffed. "Get it?"

Everyone laughed.

Smiling broadly, Fern said, "All right, all right. Let's get back to the riddle. Where does Hestia reign and Demeter rule?"

"Home and — farm?" Ivy offered tentatively.

The women got quiet as they continued to pass the food and ponder the first part of the clue.

"Hey." Jasmine was the first to speak. "Have you all forgotten this was a trip down memory lane? Who had a farm when you were kids, Mom?"

Fern frowned. "No one that I can remember."

"It says here," Violet read from her phone, "agriculture is the practice of cultivating plants and livestock."

"Well, no one in the family raised livestock," Fern said.

"No." Holly's eyes lit up, "but Mom, Dad and Grandpa had a huge vegetable garden in the backyard at our house in Kingsdale."

Fern's face slowly transformed into a smile at the memory. "So, we're talking about the garden at our childhood home?"

Holly nodded. "I think that's …"

"Peggy!" The angry shout was followed by a loud door slam. Everyone stopped and stared as Ron once again appeared in the doorway. Huffing and red in the face, he snarled, "Didn't I tell you to get these people the hell out of here?"

22 SUCH A MESS

All eyes focused on Ron, expressions ranging from Violet's fearful gaze to Fern's baleful scowl. After a moment, Peggy popped up out of her chair and rushed over to where he was standing.

"Ron, please ..." she begged. "Come with me to the office where we can talk privately." She reached for his arm.

"Hell, no!" He jerked his arm away and waved it in the direction of the women still seated around the island. "They're the ones who told the police I threatened Hiram Thurston."

In a soothing voice, Peggy said, "Ron, please calm ..."

"Don't tell me to calm down." Ron pointed a finger just an inch from Peggy's nose. "This is all your fault. If you had gotten rid of them when I told you to, I wouldn't have spent the last two hours talking to that fathead Jaworski."

Ron swiftly pivoted and walked over, placing his hands on the island countertop. He leaned forward in a menacing posture. "Which of you bitches told the police I threatened Hiram Thurston?"

Fern got to her feet. "I did. What are you going to do about it?"

"I should have known it was you, Fern." Ron stood up

straight and laughed. "Well, this won't be the first time I had you thrown out of this house."

"You can go to hell, Ron. I'm not leaving until my daughters get the inheritance Aunt Peg left them."

Ron jerked his head back, his brow furrowed. "What are you talking about? My mother didn't leave you or your spawn a dime."

"Ron," Peggy's tone was pleading. "I'm begging you. Come with me to the office to talk."

Ron continued to glare at Fern, then slowly turned to face Peggy. "What the hell have you done?"

Peggy appeared on the verge of tears. "Please …"

Ron threw his hands up in the air. "That does it! This is the final straw, Peg. Tomorrow I'm moving in here with Beverly and our son and you can start packing your bags. That is, unless you want me to have you committed for incompetency."

"Hold on, just a minute." Jasmine now got to her feet.

Ron turned and looked Jasmine up and down. "And who the hell are you?"

"I'm the Assistant DA for Dade County Florida." Jasmine walked up to Ron and mimicking him, pointed her finger and inch from his nose. "And I'm your sister's lawyer."

Ron let out a surly laugh. "You think you can go up against me, little girl?"

"No." The corners of Jasmine's mouth turned downward as she slowly shook her head. "No, I *know* I can." She held up her cellphone. "And I have Detective Jaworski on speed dial. I suggest you leave here. Now. Wouldn't look too good for you to have a domestic violence call against you — you know — seeing as how you're the prime suspect in a murder investigation."

Ron's face grew redder and he made a move toward Jasmine. "Why I ought to …"

"Ah-ah-ah, Ron," Jasmine waved her index finger in caution. "You don't want to threaten an officer of the law. I already have enough to file a restraining order against you."

Ron stopped and stood, clenching and unclenching his fists. After a moment he shuddered, turned and headed to the door. "You'll regret this, Peggy," he growled as he rushed past her out into the hall.

No one moved until they heard the door slam shut. Still facing the doorway, Peggy covered her face with her hands and began to weep.

Ivy was the first to reach her. She put an arm around her waist. "Come, Peggy. Sit down."

Violet pulled out a chair as Ivy guided her over. Fern grabbed a box of tissues from the kitchen counter.

Holly looked at Jasmine. "Nice work, Counselor."

"Thanks. Now you go lock the front door and I'll check the patio and side doors."

When they both returned to the kitchen, Peggy appeared a bit calmer. Violet, Ivy and Fern surrounded her. After a few residual sniffles, she grabbed a tissue and blew her nose.

"I'm so, so sorry," she said. "I just wanted this weekend to be — I don't know — I wanted it …"

"To be like old times, right, Peggy?" Holly said. "Like when we were kids."

Peggy nodded.

"So, the treasure hunt was your idea, not your mother's," Fern said softly.

Peggy nodded again as the tears began to roll down her cheeks. "I have more money than I can ever spend in my lifetime. I just wanted to bring the family all back together, but now everything is such a mess. What have I done?"

23 AN UNEXPECTED VISITOR

"Peggy, you did bring us back together," Holly said. "This murder is not your fault."

"But Ron ..." Peggy lowered her head once more.

Before anyone could provide another word of consolation, the doorbell rang. Peggy's head snapped up. "Who could that be? I just can't ..."

"Relax. I'll get rid of whoever it is," Jasmine said and headed to the hallway. Holly followed.

Jasmine peeked through the peephole. "Some guy. You know him?" She moved aside so Holly could take a look.

"Ugh! Yes, we met him at the memorial service. I don't remember his name."

"Should we let him in?"

Holly bit her lip as she considered the question. The doorbell rang again.

"Okay. Let's at least see what he wants."

Jasmine twisted the deadbolt and pulled the door open. "Can I help you?"

The man appeared confused as he eyed Jasmine. When his gaze shifted to Holly, a smile of recognition lit his face.

"Hello. We met at Mrs. Lowe's memorial service yesterday. You're Peggy's cousin, Holly. Or is it Ivy?"

"You were right the first time. I'm Holly, but you'll have to forgive me. I don't remember your name."

"I'm Fred Locksley, the Vice President ..." Fred let out a half-cough, half-chuckle as he said, "soon to be President of the Board of Trustees at the Country Club."

Holly grimaced as once again the word *smarmy* came to mind. Locksley appeared even oilier than this morning. Was he actually celebrating his ascension to the presidency before Hiram was even laid to rest?

"And who's this?" Fred turned his leering face back to Jasmine.

"This is my niece, Jasmine Brennan."

"*Enchanté.*" Fred reached for Jasmine's hand, but she swiftly crossed her arms in front of her.

"Is there something you wanted, Mr. Locksley?" she asked, her icy tone countering his overture.

Slightly flustered by the rebuff, Fred's smile evaporated as he pulled back his hand. "Well, yes. I was wondering if I might see Peggy."

"Peggy is indisposed at the moment," Holly intervened.

"But I really would like to ..."

"She's not receiving visitors, Mr. Locksley." Jasmine's expression reminded Holly of Nick's stony-faced stares.

"But ..."

"We'll let her know you dropped by." Jasmine reached for the door. "I'm sure she knows how to get in touch with you."

Fred Locksley's eyes grew wide as the door closed.

"You're a little bit scary, you know," Holly said.

Jasmine waggled her head. "You don't get to be assistant DA by playing nice." She turned the lock. "What do you think he really wanted?"

"Good question." Holly glanced up at the ceiling. "I vaguely remember there was a bit of tension between him and Hiram." She shook her head. "I can't remember exactly what was said. Let's go see if Ivy does."

"Who was that?" Peggy asked when they returned to the kitchen.

"Fred Locksley."

"Yuck!" was Peggy's response. "What did he want?"

"He wanted to see you, but I sent him packing," Jasmine replied.

"Yeah," Holly tilted her head in Jasmine's direction. "This one can be rather intimidating."

Peggy smiled for the first time since Ron's arrival and hasty departure. "Thank you, Jasmine." Her smile faded. "You were so brave to confront Ron the way you did."

The young lawyer waved her arm dismissively.

After a moment, Peggy shook her head. "I suppose Fred just wanted gossip — straight from the horse's mouth. That way he could go back to the Board and tell them all the gory details about Hiram's death."

"Yeah, I remember there was a brief exchange between him and Hiram at the memorial service," Holly said. "Ivy, I was wondering if you remember what it was about."

"Locksley was the skinny, *enchanté* guy with the oily hair, right?" Ivy asked.

Holly chuckled. "That's him."

Ivy squinted for a moment, then snapped her fingers. "Now I remember. Locksley said something like 'we're going to miss you when you retire'. If I remember correctly, Hiram started to object, saying he wasn't retiring, but then that woman interrupted him, and Hiram made his apologies and left."

"That's right." Holly nodded. "And just now Fred seemed to be a tad gleeful that he was about to become President of the Board of Trustees."

"So, this Locksley is someone who benefits by Hiram's death." Jasmine mused.

"Don't they say criminals always return to the scene of the crime?" Violet asked.

Jasmine grinned as she reached for her phone. "Excuse me," she said, heading to the hall. "There's a certain detective I need to call."

24 AN ETHICAL QUESTION

Ivy reached for the plastic bottle on her nightstand and pumped a dollop of moisturizer onto her hand. "Do you think Peggy's really in danger?" she asked after Holly told her about Kate's phone call.

Holly's shoulders slumped. "Look, you were with me the last time Kate's grandmother sent a warning from Spook Central."

"Yeah, she was right on the money that time." Ivy frowned.

Holly dropped down on her bed. "So, the question is what kind of danger is she in. Is she in mortal danger from the murderer? Or is she in danger of being thrown out of her home by Ron, who, coincidentally, might also be the murderer? All I know is I don't see how we can leave until we're sure she's safe. And I don't see how that can happen until this murder is solved."

Ivy nodded. "You're right. I wish this had happened before Don and Georgette left on their cruise," she said, snuggling back into her pillows. Suddenly she sprang back up. "You don't think they did it and then left town, do you?"

Holly stared at her sister. "Oh, that would be horrible, wouldn't it?" After a moment she shook her head. "No. Don seems to really care about Peggy. Even if I could believe he killed

Hiram, I can't believe he'd plant the body here for her to deal with."

"Yeah. And Georgette seems like a real sweetheart too," Ivy said, lying back down. "You don't honestly think Locksley had something to do with the murder," Ivy said, skepticism in her voice. "I don't know. He just seems too — I can't think of the right word."

"Too spineless?" Holly grinned.

"Yeah, that's it." Ivy nodded. "I can see him being devious and sneaky, but I don't see him having the nerve to actually murder someone."

"Hmm." Holly pulled the bedcovers down and got in bed. "I'd love to know what that woman said to Hiram after the memorial service. Seemed like he had all the time in the world for Peggy, but after the woman spoke with him, he ended our conversation and left pretty abruptly."

"Oh boy!" Ivy moved to the edge of the bed. "I just remembered something."

"What?"

"Locksley tried to hear what the woman was saying. He got so close that Hiram actually bumped into him when he turned around."

Holly chuckled. "Yeah. That was pretty funny."

"So, you think whatever that exchange was about had something to do with Hiram's murder?"

A soft knock on the door prevented her from answering. Ivy walked over and opened the door.

"We didn't wake you, did we?" Violet asked apologetically.

"No," Ivy said. "We were just talking about Fred Locksley. Come in."

Holly sat up and gestured to the edge of the bed. "Have

a seat. What's on your mind?" she asked. "Discussing the murder?"

"No." Violet shook her head. "It's more of an ethical question we have," she said. "You know, a question of right and wrong."

"Oh, for God's sake, Vy." Jasmine shook her head impatiently. "Just get to the point." Turning to Holly and Ivy, she said, "She thinks it's immoral for us to take the money from Aunt Peggy. What do you think?"

"Oh," Holly said, slowly exhaling through her lips.

"What does your mother say?" Ivy asked.

Violet sighed. "That's just it. She told me not to be stupid. She says we didn't come all this way for nothing, and if Peggy wants to give us the money, we should just take it. But I don't feel right about it."

"What do you say, Jasmine?" Holly asked.

It was Jasmine's turn to sigh. "Look, I could really use that money. I have to admit, I had no qualms about inheriting the money from Great Aunt Peg. But now it seems as if Peggy is paying us to get together and spend time with her. I don't feel quite as good about that."

"May I offer my opinion?" Ivy asked.

"Please do," Violet said. "That's why we came to you. We know our mother is just looking out for us, but we really want to know what you think."

"First of all," Ivy began, "I think the fact that you're even looking at this as a question of ethics speaks volumes about your character."

Holly nodded and smiled in agreement.

"Secondly," Ivy continued, "You are both young and you can put this money to good use. You, Violet, for your children, and you, Jasmine, to get out from under the burden of your school loans. I've watched you interact with Peggy these last few days, and I don't think it was just because of the money."

"Oh no," Violet said. "I really like her."

"Me too," Jasmine added. "I feel bad for her. Except for that other brother, Don, she seems so alone. What? Did Great Aunt Peg keep her locked up here?"

"That wouldn't surprise me," Holly replied, "but let me ask you a question. If Peggy said she'd like to come to Florida for a visit, what would you do?"

"Oh, that would be great," Violet smiled. "In fact, tomorrow I'm going to invite her."

"We could take her shopping for some new clothes," Jasmine snickered.

"Well, there you go," Holly laughed. "I can tell you this. The Lowes were very rich, so like she said, she has all the money she needs. Clearly, the money means nothing to Peggy, but *you* do."

"That's right," Ivy said. "Having you in her life is what will enrich hers."

Jasmine rubbed her palms together. "Okay then. I'm glad that's settled. Now as a show of good faith, I think the least we can do is work out the riddle and finish the treasure hunt. I know that would make her happy."

"Geesh," Holly said. "With all these interruptions, I keep forgetting about the riddle."

"Right," Ivy said. "Before Ron burst in, wasn't Fern saying it must have something to do with the garden at our old house in Kingsdale?"

"Yes." Violet said. "But what about those crazy bonus clues?"

"I don't know about the rocks and stones thing," Holly said, "and Huck Finn is the only boy on a raft I can think of."

Ivy pursed her lips. "Maybe this will be like the first riddle. We figured out the where. Sunset. Then we figured out the rest of it when we got there."

"Yeah," Holly agreed. "Maybe after a good night's sleep, it will all fall into place once we're there."

"Hey, before we go," Jasmine said, "you mentioned you were discussing Locksley. Any more ideas about how or why he might be involved?"

Holly recounted the conversation she and Ivy had. "I'm assuming you called Jaworski. What did he say?"

Jasmine groaned. "He listened to me, but I don't think he'll even bother talking to Locksley. You know, Ron is an obnoxious bully, but that does not make him a killer. If it were me, I'd be talking to Locksley first thing tomorrow morning. But it's not my investigation, is it?"

"Isn't it?" Holly asked, a coy smile on her face.

"All right," Ivy intervened. "Let's all get some rest and pick this back up tomorrow."

She started to get up, but Violet stopped her. "We'll let ourselves out."

At the door, Jasmine stopped and looked back at Holly and Ivy in their beds. "Aren't they adorable?" she said, closing the door before the pillow Holly threw reached her.

25 ANOTHER UNEXPECTED VISITOR

"Good morning, ladies," Higgins said as Holly and Ivy entered the dining room.

"Good to see you back, Higgins," Holly said. "Welcome home."

"Yes," Ivy added. "Sorry you had to cut your visit to your sister-in-law's short."

The butler simply gave his head a slight bow and exited through the door to the kitchen.

"Good morning, Aunties," Jasmine greeted lifting up her coffee cup from where she sat at the table.

"Morning," Holly said walking over to the sideboard and lifting the cover of the first of two chafing dishes. "French toast! Yum."

"And bacon!" Ivy smiled as she held up the cover of the second chafing dish. "Perfect. I'm starved."

"Nice to have the Higginses home, isn't it?" Jasmine leaned back in her chair.

"Absolutely." Holly sat down beside Jasmine. "They must have gotten back really late."

"And still they're up serving us," Ivy said.

Holly leaned towards Jasmine conspiratorially. "Did you talk to him?"

In a low voice, Jasmine replied. "Yes. He said he and his wife locked up the house and left around two o'clock. And get this. Just as they were leaving, a man stopped by asking for Peggy."

"Locksley?" Ivy whispered wide-eyed.

Jasmine shook her head. "No. Somebody named Patrick Keefe."

Holly's head snapped to attention at the name.

"You know him?" Jasmine asked.

"Yes. When we were leaving the Country Club after the memorial service, Pat Keefe came up to us to speak to Peggy before we got in the car."

Still wide-eyed, Ivy added, "It was pretty clear there was some history between them."

"You mean romantically?" Jasmine asked, a trace of wonder in her voice.

"Good morning!" Peggy entered the dining room, smiling, even though her eyes were puffy, and she appeared unrested. "How's everyone this morning?"

"Great," Ivy said. "You look like you didn't get much sleep."

Peggy frowned and walked over to the sideboard. "Well, I did toss and turn a bit, but I fell asleep eventually — after I heard the Higginses arrive." She grabbed a plate and speared a slice of French toast.

"Good morning," Violet said as she and Fern walked in.

"That coffee smells divine." Fern headed straight to the urn and filled a cup.

Peggy sat down at the head of the table. "So, your riddle-solving got interrupted last night. I think you should resume your discussion so we can plan our day."

Holly nodded as she slid a piece of French toast through the last of the syrup on her plate. "We talked a little in our room last night and we think Fern's right. We ought to go to our child-hood home in Kingsdale."

"Yes, we think that maybe once we're there we'll figure out the other clues," Violet added.

"So will you at least confirm that we're on the right track, Peggy?" Ivy asked.

Peggy smiled. "Yes. You are on the right track."

"You think the new owners will let us on the property?" Fern asked.

Peggy's smile widened. "I own the property. I rent it out to a gardener who used to work here and is now retired."

"Well, this sounds very promising indeed!" Jasmine remarked.

At the sound of the doorbell, Jasmine put down her coffee cup and both she and Holly started to get up.

"Where are you going?" Peggy asked. "Higgins will get that."

Jasmine chuckled, dropping back down in her chair. "Good ole Higgins."

"More coffee, Aunt Peggy?" Violet asked as she got up to refill her own cup.

Holly thought Peggy couldn't have looked more touched by Violet's gesture if she said she was naming her next child after her. "Yes, please," she said, handing Violet her cup.

As she did, Higgins entered the dining room and walked over to Peggy. When he leaned close to her ear and whispered what everyone knew was the identity of the visitor who'd just rung the doorbell, her face reflected a weary resignation

"Tell her I'll be with her in a moment," Peggy said as Violet handed the coffee cup to her. "Thank you," she said, then glanced around the table. She let out a small laugh as she saw that all eyes were on her. "I suppose you want to know who's here. It's Beverly, Ron's wife."

"So, she's here to apologize for her boorish husband and play good cop," Fern said, clearly disgusted.

"Aunt Peggy, would you mind if I sit in on your conversation with her?" Jasmine asked, her tone uncharacteristically gentle.

"Oh, I don't think that's necessary," Peggy replied.

"Don't be naïve, Peggy," Fern cautioned. "You know that sleezy social climber would love to move in here even more than Ron would. You shouldn't be alone with her. You're too soft. She'll have you convinced you can't handle this place by yourself. You know she will."

"Sleezy social climber?" Beverly glared at Fern from the doorway. "Better than money-grubbing white trash."

26 HISTORY

Fern slowly got to her feet. Holly and Jasmine quickly got on either side of her as she locked eyes with Beverly.

"White trash?" Fern's mouth curled into a grim smile. "Well, I'm not the one who had to get pregnant to get my husband to marry me," Fern said with deadly calm.

Beverly's face flushed scarlet. She started to speak, but Peggy rose and said, "Beverly, let's go into the drawing room please." She moved swiftly to her sister-in-law's side, took her by the arm and led her out into the hallway.

Jasmine turned to her mother. "You all right?"

"Yes," Fern said. "Now go and, no matter what Peggy says, you stay with her until that viper leaves."

Jasmine nodded and left the room.

Fern looked at Holly. "What did you think? That I would assault her?" She sat down and returned her napkin back to her lap.

Holly cleared her throat. "Well, it was a rather intense exchange." She reached for Fern's coffee cup and went over to the urn for a refill.

Violet grimaced as she exchanged a glance with Ivy. After a few moments, Ivy looked over at Fern. "The other day when

Holly asked you if there was some history between you and Ron, you said yes." Ivy said. "Care to tell us about it?"

"Thank you," Fern said as Holly placed the coffee cup in front of her. After taking a sip, she began. "When Aunt Peg's husband died, I took the bus up here for the funeral. With Tommy gone and the girls in college, I was having a hard time making ends meet. When Aunt Peg found out I couldn't afford the airfare, she invited me to stay here and said she'd buy my plane ticket back. While I was here, she also offered to help pay tuition for Violet and Jasmine. Then Ron found out. In less than an hour, my bag was packed for me, and I was put in a taxi to the airport."

"You never told us." Violet got up and moved to the chair beside her mother, taking her hand in hers. "How awful that must have been for you."

Fern smiled weakly at her daughter. "The awful part was that, for one day, I thought I had secured my daughters' futures. To have that all evaporate in an instant — well, let's just say I cried all the way home."

"So, Aunt Peg just went along with whatever Ron said?" Ivy asked.

"Oh, she wrote me and said she was sorry that she couldn't help with the girls' tuition. She claimed she didn't know that their money was all tied up in investments when she made the offer." Fern shrugged. "Now do you understand why I believed that Aunt Peg left me and the twins something in her will?"

"Was Beverly in the picture back then?" Holly asked.

"Oh yes," Fern sneered. "Beverly Kelly was a little tramp — she and her three sisters. But they were Kingsdale's answer to the Kardashians. They knew just how to get their claws into a man, and they only went after men with money."

"Surely the Lowe's could have paid her off," Holly said.

Fern let out a laugh. "You don't remember the Kellys, do

you?"

Holly shook her head.

"The girls were tramps and their brothers were brutes. Everybody was afraid of them. From what I heard, they threatened Ron with I don't know what, but he agreed to marry Beverly without a fight."

"A shotgun wedding, huh?" Holly grinned.

"Yep," Fern nodded. "So, Miss High-and-Mighty can act like she's a class act out here with the Country Club set, but everyone in Kingsdale knows how she got where she is. I guess she's been lying for so long, she probably believes her own lies. She forgot who she was talking to when she called me white trash."

"Does Peggy know this story?" Ivy asked.

"I honestly don't know," Fern replied. "Peggy has always been good to me and kept in touch throughout the years. I feel bad now that I didn't always return her calls or letters." Fern pounded the table with her fist. "But I'll be damned if I let Ron and Beverly take advantage of her."

"Don't worry, Mom." Violet patted her mother's hand. "Our Jasmine will make sure that doesn't happen."

27 LEGAL MATTERS

Jasmine gave a light tap on the door before entering the drawing room. Beverly's expression as she stared at her was one of disbelief. Jasmine gave her a pleasant smile and sat down beside Peggy.

"Excuse me," Beverly said, not trying to hide her annoyance. "I'd like to talk to my sister-in-law in private."

"Beverly ..." Peggy began, her expression apologetic.

Jasmine patted her aunt's knee, "Mrs. Lowe, I'm my Aunt Peggy's lawyer and adviser, so I need to be present for any discussions regarding legal matters."

"This is a personal — a family matter." Beverly gave her hand a dismissive wave. "This doesn't concern you."

"Is it about the disposition of this house and property?" Jasmine asked.

Beverly glared at Jasmine whose smile hadn't altered.

Peggy sighed. "Beverly, why don't you just tell us why you're here?"

"Us?"

When neither Peggy nor Jasmine replied, Beverly gave her head a shake. Later Jasmine would relate to Holly that it was as if she realized she'd lost this argument — that she had to hit reset and shift tactics if she was going to accomplish her purpose in coming here. When the sister-in-law looked back at Peggy, her features softened.

"Peggy, you know how much you mean to *us*." She shot a toxic glance at Jasmine. "Me and Ron that is. And look, I know Ron lost his temper last night. He told me all about what happened and he's really sorry." Here she paused as if waiting for approval. When neither Peggy, nor Jasmine, reacted, she inhaled deeply and continued. "Peggy, don't you think that this house is just — well, just a bit too much for you to handle?"

"What makes you think that?" Peggy asked.

Her sister-in-law pulled her head back slightly, surprised by the question. "Well, you're all by yourself. How will you manage?"

"You may not realize it, but I've been managing the property for years. My mother turned all financial matters over to me. I paid the bills and handled her investments."

"You did?" Beverly appeared disconcerted by this information. Again, she waved her hand as if she were brushing away a pesky insect. "But surely you can't manage the staff. Why they'll just ride roughshod over an old mai ... over a single woman."

Peggy frowned. "Clearly you and Ron weren't aware of this, but I handled not just the house and grounds staff, which included hiring and firing. I also retained and supervised any repairman we needed, and I managed all of mother's pet construction projects like the koi pond and the garden shed."

At this, Beverly just stared at Peggy as if she were looking at a stranger. "Well, I find this all ..."

"Surprising?" Peggy said.

Beverly's hands formed fists in her lap, and she ran her fingers along her palms nervously. "I — we just didn't know all that."

The plastic smile Jasmine had adopted to annoy Beverly earlier had transformed into a genuinely amused grin. She, too, was surprised by Peggy's revelations. Peggy was nobody's push-over, and her sister-in-law was not prepared for the formidable woman she'd so clearly under-estimated. After a moment, Beverly again switched gears.

"But Peggy, with your mother gone, you can't really want to stay here all by yourself. I mean, the place will be full of memories that may haunt you. Wouldn't you rather get a fresh start somewhere new?"

Peggy let out a small laugh. "Oh, Beverly, you really don't know anything about me, do you? I've lived here since I was fifteen years old. My stepfather treated me like his daughter, and I loved him the same as my father. I know my mother could be harsh with others, but not with me. I have only good memories here in this house, so no, I'm not worried about anyone haunting me."

"Still, you might be lonely. What if Ron and I move in with …"

"No," Peggy said with force. "Even this house isn't big enough for the three of us."

Beverly's eyelids narrowed to slits, giving her face a reptilian quality. "But what about real life threats? Like whoever planted Hiram's body here in the house. A woman alone can fall prey to all sorts of villains. She needs male protection. And let's face it. You don't have any prospects."

"As a matter of fact, I do," Peggy said with a satisfied smile.

"You do?" Beverly jerked her head back in surprise, but quickly recovered. "Are you considering Fred Locksley?"

"Oh, hell no," Peggy scoffed.

"Then who?"

Peggy crossed her arms in front of her. "Pat Keefe."

"You can't be serious," Beverly scoffed. "Pat Keefe is no prospect for you. Ron would never allow you to marry him."

Jasmine put a reassuring hand on her aunt's forearm. "Ms. Lowe, Aunt Peggy is well over the age of consent. She doesn't need her brother's permission to marry."

Beverly glared at Jasmine with a look that could have soured milk. "I wasn't talking to you." Turning back to Peggy she softened her expression. "What if we just temporarily move in with …"

"Absolutely not," Peggy said, her voice calm, with a touch of steel.

This time, Beverly recognized defeat. She clutched her handbag and got to her feet. "I'm sorry you feel that way, Peggy," she said, heading to the door. As she reached for the doorknob, she turned. "If you change your mind …"

"Yes, I know how to reach you." Peggy nodded. "You can see yourself out, can't you?"

Beverly simply scowled as she opened the door and left.

"You didn't need me after all," Jasmine smiled as she squeezed Peggy's hand. "Hey, why are you trembling?"

"I can't believe I said exactly what I wanted to say! I wasn't nervous — until now," Peggy laughed. "You know I was only able to face her down because you were sitting right next to me."

Jasmine chuckled. "To paraphrase a famous line, 'you had the power in you all the time'." She stood up and offered Peggy her hand. "Now let's go tell the others. They're gonna love this."

28 THE TREASURE

On the drive to Kingsdale, laughter filled the mini-van as Jasmine recounted Peggy and Beverly's meeting. She mimicked Beverly's expressions to everyone's delight.

"Yep," she said. "You could practically see the wheels in her head spinning as Aunt Peggy shot down every one of her arguments for why she should give up the house. It was like watching Serena Williams return an amateur tennis player's serves. Every one an ace."

"Oh, stop," Peggy smiled, glancing at Jasmine in the rear-view mirror, clearly pleased with the compliment.

"All I know is I'd love to be a fly on the wall at Ron and Beverly's house right now," Fern said.

"Oh, I don't know." Peggy shrugged. "I almost feel sorry for them."

"Bite your tongue!" Fern snapped.

Peggy laughed at the horrified expression on Fern's face. "Relax. I said 'almost'."

"I'm with Fern on this one," Ivy said from the back of the van. "I'm sure they're plotting another approach to get you out of your house. You can bet they're not going to give up."

"And neither is Peggy," Holly said. "So, let's forget about

them and focus on our mission today. Violet, remind us of those bonus clues again."

For the rest of the drive to the Donnelly homestead, the women mulled over possible meanings for the clues.

"Kingsdale, one mile," Ivy read the road sign. "I'm so excited. I was only 6-years old when we moved. But I have such vivid memories of this place. I wonder if it's changed much."

"The street we lived on has seen some changes," Peggy replied as she flipped on the turn signal. "Someone finally built a house on the vacant lot across from our houses. But I've tried to keep your place the same as it was back when you lived there."

"What about your house, Peggy?" Holly asked. "It was right next door."

"I would have bought it, but unfortunately it burned down. I sold the lot and new owners built a more modern house on it." Peggy made a turn onto a two-lane road. Around a curve the road sloped upward.

"Oh boy," Ivy said, unable to contain the excitement in her voice. "How many times did we walk up and down this hill? Remember, Holly? Oh gosh, I just had a memory of us — you, too, Fern — walking to the movies in Luzerne. Remember we used to go to Saturday matinees?"

"Yes, I remember," Holly said, her smile as wide as her sister's. "But you need to calm down or you might pass out by the time we get to the house."

"Look at all these houses." Ivy ignored Holly's caution. "None of these were here when we were kids. "Look, look. The Town Hall and the Firehouse haven't changed a bit."

"No," Fern said, "but I like the new sign out front. Boy, I remember the Firemen's picnic every summer. That's where I met your father, girls."

The twins bombarded their mother with questions about

their parents' courtship as Peggy drove to Kingsdale Street.

"Here we are," she said, turning onto a gravel driveway beside a white house with a cozy front porch. "Mr. Costello said he wouldn't be home this morning, so we can explore the yard on our own."

"Beautiful!" Ivy exclaimed as she got out of the van. "Just like I remembered it." She walked over to her cousin and threw her arms around her in a tight embrace. "Thank you, Peggy."

Peggy appeared to be aglow as Ivy released her. "Okay, now. Remember why you're here."

"Right," Fern said. "Let's go out back to where the garden was." She led the way past an apple and cherry tree.

"Could these be the same trees we used to climb?" Holly asked.

"No," Peggy replied. "Those trees had to come down, but I replanted a Macintosh apple and a Bing cherry tree in their place about fifteen years ago."

Not stopping, Fern continued to a 15' x 20' patch of ground in the left corner of the yard. Sprouts were poking through the rich dark soil. "Looks like your tenant has quite a garden started," she said.

"And in exactly the same spot where Mom and Dad had their vegetable garden." Holly reached down and rubbed her hand across the dark, rich soil. "Beautiful."

"Yes, Mr. Costello is quite a gardener, and his wife cans everything," Peggy said. "Not many people like them around anymore."

Ivy looked around and sighed. "The only difference from when we were kids is that shed in the corner there. Quite a beautiful shed, isn't it?"

"Yeah, yeah," Fern said, a trace of impatience in her voice, "but what are we supposed to be looking for?" She scanned the garden bed, her brow furrowed. "Violet, what was that about sticks and stones?"

"Not sticks and stones," Violet corrected. "Rocks and stones don't hurt my bones."

Ivy snapped her fingers. "I know!" She ran over to the shed and disappeared behind it. Fern and Holly followed.

When Violet and Jasmine arrived, they found the three sisters, standing still, staring at a low-growing shrub sprouting up from a four-foot expanse of rocky ground. The shrub was in full bloom, covered in white bell-shaped flowers.

"Okaaaay," Jasmine said. "What are we looking at?"

Fern pointed. "The shrub that's growing in that rocky soil."

"Get it?" Holly poked Jasmine in the ribs. "Rocks and stones won't hurt my bones."

"It's a berry bush." Ivy brushed her hand across the leaves. "I remember our teeth used to turn blue when we ate them. Blueberries!"

"Huckleberries! Holly said excitedly. "So the boy on the raft — that was Huck Finn."

Peggy came up alongside Holly wearing a big grin. "So, you've done it. You've found the treasure."

"We know it's a huckleberry bush," Violet said, "but there's just one thing. We haven't figured out what the clue, 'carton', means?"

"Oh, I'll give you that one," Peggy said. "The plant is a Box Huckleberry."

"Oh, I get it," Jasmine groaned. "Carton. Box. You're such a joker, Aunt Peggy." Everyone laughed as she landed a soft punch on Peggy's arm.

"But why is this plant a treasure?" Fern asked, clearly puzzled.

"Because it's an endangered plant in Pennsylvania," Peggy replied, "and now we get to report it to the Pennsylvania Department of Conservation and Natural Resources. We'll be able to apply for heritage status for the property. The Box Huckleberry is our family treasure."

"Oh, Peggy!" Ivy once again threw her arms around her cousin. "*You* are the family treasure."

29 A TRIP DOWN MEMORY LANE

"What are you two up to?" Fern asked as she walked over to the mini-van where Holly and Ivy were talking quietly.

Holly smiled. "Remember Pat Keefe?"

"Of course. I was friends with his sister Irene. She told me Pat had a thing for Peggy. That was way back in grade school."

"I knew it," Holly said. "Well, we ran into him when we were leaving the Country Club after the memorial service."

"He said if we got to Kingsdale to drop in for a visit," Ivy added. "We asked Peggy to tell us about him, but she just said there was nothing to tell."

"We want to drive past the Keefe house," Holly said. "Pat told us he's usually sitting out on the porch now that he's retired."

Ivy smiled, wiggling her ring finger. "And he's a widower."

"The only problem is we don't think Peggy will drive by Pat's even if we ask her to." Holly frowned.

Fern glanced over at the spot in the front yard where Peggy was explaining something about the house to Jasmine and Violet. "Why don't you just offer to drive?"

"Great idea," Holly smiled and peeked inside the van. "The

keys are in the ignition." She opened the door and climbed in the driver's seat as Fern walked around and got in the front passenger side.

As Ivy slid open the side door and climbed in back, Peggy and the twins walked over.

Holly lowered her window. "Hey, Peggy. Nick and I were thinking about buying a mini-van. Would you mind letting me take a test drive? I'd just like to see what it feels like."

Peggy shrugged. "Sure. Why not?" She got in and took the seat Holly had previously occupied.

Holly sneaked a side glance at Fern, who smiled and turned to look out the window. "Hey, since we're here, why don't we take a drive around town?"

"Around town?" Jasmine said. "You told us there are a total of four main streets and four cross streets in all of Kingsdale. Haven't we already covered half the town?"

"That's right," Fern agreed. "So it won't take long at all."

"Oh, I'd really love that," Ivy said.

Holly turned the key in the ignition. "Okay, then. Let's roll."

Holly backed out of the driveway and headed up the hill. For the next ten minutes, Ivy and Fern pointed to the various houses, remembering who lived in them back when they were children. Peggy confirmed if the same families still occupied the homes, or who the new owners were.

When they reached Flannagan Street, Holly flipped on her turn signal.

"No, don't go this way," Peggy said.

"Why not?" Holly asked as she made the turn.

"I think they're doing some road repair work up ahead." Peggy moved to the edge of her seat. "You'll have to make the next right back down Kingsdale Street."

When they reached the stop sign at the intersection of Kingsdale and Flannagan Streets, Fern said, "I don't see any road work ahead."

"No, you can't see it from here," Peggy said nervously, "but there is …"

"Hey, isn't that the Keefes' house there, Peggy?" Holly pointed to the third house on the block.

"He's the guy we met after the memorial service, right, Peggy?" Ivy asked from the back seat. Not giving Peggy a chance to reply, she continued. "Holly, why don't you just pull over and let's see if he's home."

"I don't think this is a good idea," Peggy said shaking her head.

"Why not? He told us to stop in if we came to Kingsdale," Holly said.

"Yes, and I'd love to see Pat," Fern added. "I'd really like to hear what Irene's been up to."

Peggy sank back in her seat as Holly pulled up across the street from the Keefe house. Holly and Fern got out first and began to cross the street. As they did, the front door of the house opened and Pat Keefe stepped outside, a big smile on his face.

"So, you made it to Kingsdale?" he said.

"Yes, we've been taking a trip down memory lane." Holly crossed the street.

"Great. Come on up and have a seat on the porch. I'll go in and get some lemonade. I just made it."

Holly and Fern mounted the steps as Ivy, Peggy and the twins got out of the van. Peggy stayed back as Violet and Ivy crossed the street.

Jasmine started to cross, but when Peggy didn't move, she

turned to face her. "Hey, Aunt Peggy, didn't you tell Beverly that Pat Keefe was a prospect?"

"Shh," Peggy grabbed her niece's arm. "I just said that to shut her up. Please, Jasmine, don't tell anyone I said that."

"Okay. I won't. I promise," Jasmine reassured her. "But c'mon. We can't just stand here."

Still Peggy didn't move. She looked up at the Keefe house and bit the corner of her lip. Jasmine gave her arm a little tug. After a moment, Peggy took a deep breath, shook her head and let Jasmine lead her across the street. Just as they mounted the top step, Pat appeared in the doorway with a tray of glasses and a pitcher of lemonade.

"Here, let me get the door for you," Jasmine said.

The moment she released Peggy's arm, Peggy scurried across the porch and squeezed in between Holly and Ivy on the glider.

"So, Pat, do you remember me?" Fern asked.

"Sure do. You were friends with my sister, Irene," Pat replied as he started to pour lemonade into the glasses on the tray. "I remember you two used to chase me out when you wanted to play your 45's and talk about boys."

Fern laughed. "Oh, to be that young again. How is Irene by the way?"

The conversation drifted pleasantly from one memory to the next as they sipped their lemonade and Pat answered questions about old neighbors and friends. Even Jasmine and Violet had questions about what their mother and aunts were like when they were kids.

"This is so nice, Pat," Fern said. "I do remember sitting on this porch, sharing secrets with Irene. In fact, I have to ask you. Is that the same glider from back then?"

Pat laughed. "Sure is. I keep the hinges well oiled. They

don't make 'em like they used to." He turned his gaze to Peggy. "You're awfully quiet, Peg. You remember sitting with me on the glider, don't you?"

Peggy, who appeared to have achieved a level of calm wedged between her two cousins, caught her breath. "Um — vaguely," she said as her cheeks turned a pale pink.

"Whoa!" Jasmine grinned. "Pat and Peggy sittin' on a tree. K-i-s-s-i-n-g."

The pink in Peggy's cheeks changed to scarlet as she glared at Jasmine.

Pat aimed a gentle smile at Peggy as he reached for the pitcher. "More lemonade anyone?" While he refilled glasses, a car drove up and parked in front of the mini-van.

"I wonder who that is," Pat said looking across the street. "Some days not a single car drives by and today, I get two visitors. Will wonders never cease?"

The women all turned their attention as the car door opened.

"Oh no," Peggy said under her breath as Detective Jaworski got out.

All conversation ceased. Pat put the pitcher down as Jaworski sauntered across the street. When he reached the top step, he glanced over at the women. "Well, isn't this cozy," he said, an unpleasant smile on his face. No one said a word. He turned to face Pat.

"Are you Patrick Keefe?"

"Yes."

"I'd like to ask you some questions, Mr. Keefe," Jaworski sneered, "that is, if you can break away from your harem here."

Pat appeared unfazed by the snide comment. "Questions about what?" he asked.

"The murder of Hiram Thurston."

"Why would you want to talk to me about that?" Pat asked in a calm, even voice.

"Two witnesses put you at the scene of the crime hours before the body was discovered. And another witness says you had a violent argument with Mr. Thurston the week before he was murdered," Jaworski smirked. "That's why."

30 BACK HOME

Holly took the wheel and for the first ten minutes of the drive home no one spoke. When they reached the highway, she finally broke the silence.

"That Jaworski is a rather unpleasant fellow, isn't he?" she said.

"Spoken like a true English major," Jasmine scoffed. "Look, he's no worse than most of the law enforcement types I deal with. You know, he wouldn't be doing his job if he didn't question Pat. Just the fact that the Higginses said he was at the house required him to question him."

"Sound familiar, Holly?" Ivy laughed.

"Yep," Holly replied. "Jasmine, you sound just like my husband, Nick. You know he's a detective?"

"No!" Jasmine said, her eyes wide in disbelief. "How did we not discuss this before? When can I meet this guy?"

Before Holly could reply, Peggy turned to Jasmine. "I want to know who said they saw Pat argue with Hiram?"

Jasmine hesitated, looking a bit uncomfortable. "Listen. I sat in on the interview with Pat as a courtesy. I told him it would be a conflict of interest for me to represent him and you and recommended he find his own lawyer. Still, I feel an obligation to keep confidential what was discussed with Jaworski."

"Seriously?" Peggy said, clearly annoyed.

"Seriously." Jasmine replied.

"It had to be someone at the Country Club," Peggy said looking out the window. "Don't worry. I'll find out who it was."

"I take it you don't think Pat murdered Hiram," Holly said.

"And put his body in my library?" Peggy's voice rose an octave. "Absolutely not!"

****

As they pulled up in front of the house, Holly looked in the rearview mirror. "I think you have a visitor, Peggy."

"I don't want to see anyone," Peggy said as Jasmine slid the side door of the van open and got out. Peggy quickly followed and headed to the front door.

"Peggy!" a man's voice called out.

Peggy groaned when she turned and spotted Fred Locksley. She shook her head and started up the stairs as the others piled out of the van. Locksley tried to hurry past, but Jasmine caught him by the arm.

"Mr. Locksley, Peggy doesn't want to see anyone right now," she said.

"But I want to talk to her." Locksley whined, not his usual ingratiating self. "Look, here she comes."

Everyone stopped to stare as Peggy walked back towards them, her fists clenched, a determined expression on her face.

Locksley pulled his arm loose from Jasmine's light grasp and tried to reach for Peggy's hand. "Peggy, dear. I've been so worried about you."

Peggy moved back just out of reach. "Can it, Fred. I want to know one thing. Did you tell the police that Pat Keefe had an argument with Hiram Thurston? A violent argument?"

Locksley's face reflected uncertainty, as if he were struggling to decide what answer Peggy wanted to hear.

"Well, Fred?" Peggy glared at him. "It's a simple yes or no question."

"Well, uh, yes, I did. I mean he could be the killer, and I had to tell the truth," he said with tepid conviction. "Didn't I?"

Peggy moved closer to Locksley, who now took a step back. "Pat Keefe is no killer." She jabbed her finger in his chest. "And if I find out you lied, I'll skin you alive myself."

Satisfied with the look of horror on Locksley's face, Peggy pivoted and retraced her steps to the front door. Fern and Ivy followed.

"It's best you leave," Holly said to the stricken man as she and Jasmine turned and headed inside.

Locksley stood staring. As the front door of the mansion closed, his cellphone sounded his ringtone, "Hail to the Chief".

"You've assembled everything we need at the Temple?" he asked. "No, no. Tonight is the full moon. We must go through with the ceremony no matter what." Fred listened for a few moments. "Yes. Nothing will stop me from being inducted as Supreme Commander. I'll be at the Country Club at 11:00 P.M. sharp."

Fred slipped his phone back in his jacket pocket and walked to his car. As he drove off, Violet lifted herself up from the floor of the mini-van where she'd been searching for her cellphone and watched as his car disappeared down the drive.

31 FEELINGS

Fern and Ivy stood waiting in the main entry hall when Holly and Jasmine arrived inside.

"Where's Peggy?" Holly asked.

Ivy grimaced. "She said she was going into the office, and she wanted to be left alone."

"I've never seen her like this," Fern said. "Holly, why don't you go talk to her?"

"Me?"

"Yes, you," Ivy said. "You know very well you're the one she looks up to. If you can't get her to talk, no one can."

"Hmpf," was all Holly managed to utter in reply.

"Go get her, Champ." Jasmine landed a playful punch on her upper arm.

Releasing an audible sigh, Holly headed to the office. She stood outside for a moment, then tapped lightly on the door.

"Go away," Peggy said.

"Peggy, it's me, Holly. Please. May I come in and talk with you?"

"I'm sorry, Holly, but I'd rather be alone."

"If that were true, you wouldn't have invited us all here for a family reunion." When she got no response, Holly continued. "You didn't have sisters, Peggy, and you're probably used to handling things all by yourself. But you don't have to anymore. You've got cousins."

Holly lowered her head and waited, hoping she'd hit the right note. When Peggy still did not reply, she finally turned, recognizing defeat. She only took a few steps, when the door opened and a tearful Peggy sniffed, "Please come in."

Peggy dropped into one of two leather chairs positioned in front of the desk, covered her face with her hands and sobbed. "Oh, Holly. I — I just don't know what to do."

Holly sat down in the chair across from her cousin and gave her shoulder a squeeze. "About what?" she asked gently.

Peggy dabbed at her eyes with a tissue, then blew her nose. "You're right. I am used to handling things on my own. Normally, I can deal with anything, but right now I don't understand why I feel so frustrated and angry and ..."

"Emotional?"

"Yes," Peggy nodded. "That's it."

"Could it be because of your feelings for Pat?"

Peggy looked at Holly with an expression so forlorn, Holly winced.

"Am I that obvious?" Peggy asked.

"Not just you. It was pretty clear that Pat has feelings for you too," Holly said.

"You think so?"

"Are you kidding?" Holly asked. "The way he looked at you. Absolutely."

Peggy shook her head. "You just don't know ..."

"Then tell me," Holly said. "What happened between you

two?"

Peggy inhaled deeply and began. "We were, what I guess you'd call, childhood sweethearts. When my mother remarried, we moved from Kingsdale out here. Pat and I kept in touch by phone. Sometimes, I'd pretend I wanted to visit one of my girlfriends from the old neighborhood, and Don would drive me to Kingsdale. As soon as I got dropped off, I'd meet Pat at a pre-arranged spot, and we'd go to the movies. Or, like he said, just sit on the glider and talk for hours."

"That sounds so sweet," Holly said. "What happened?"

"When I turned sixteen, my mother wanted to throw a Sweet Sixteen bash at the Country Club. I invited Pat. The next day my mother told me I could never see him again. She said he was not good enough for the daughter of Ronald Lowe. No matter how I begged, she wouldn't let me see him. And she wouldn't let me go to Kingsdale without her."

"So, you never spoke to Pat since your Sweet Sixteen?" Holly asked. "Didn't you try to call him?"

"I wanted to, but ..." Peggy burst into tears.

Holly got up and grabbed a box of tissues on the mahogany credenza behind the desk. She handed the box to Peggy. After drying her eyes, she finally said, "I found out my stepfather paid Pat to stay away from me. There was no point in trying to call after that."

"And you never ran into Pat again?"

"No. I couldn't go to Kingsdale, and I certainly wasn't going to run into him at the Country Club. Pat's a year older than I am. A year later, I heard he joined the Navy. A few years later, at one of my class reunions, someone told me he got married."

Holly sat back, her eyes reduced to slits. "You say you 'found out' your stepfather paid off Pat. Who told you that?"

Peggy's brow furrowed as she tried to remember. After a

moment she replied. "Ron."

Holly shrugged. "You sure he was telling the truth. Did you ever ask your stepfather about it?"

Peggy sniffed. "No. I was so hurt. I felt so betrayed by Pat that I didn't ever want to talk about it."

"Well, based on how Pat reacted when he saw you after the memorial service and again today, I think he really cares for you."

Peggy locked eyes with Holly, her expression pained and world-weary. "But how do I know that he didn't come looking for me now just because my mother's dead? Tell me, Holly, how do I know he's not just after my money?"

"Ah," Holly nodded. "That's a tough question. One I can't answer. All I know is, you still have feelings for this man, and based on what I've observed, he has feelings for you. You've jumped to his defense and don't believe he had anything to do with Hiram's murder. For heaven's sake, you even threatened to flay Fred Locksley if he lied about the argument between Pat and Hiram."

Peggy let out a small laugh. "I did, didn't I?"

"Yes, you did." Holly smiled and tapped Peggy's knee. "So, I think you should ask Pat point blank if he took money from your stepfather. What's the worst that can happen?"

Peggy frowned. "I guess the worst has already happened."

"That's right. And I think Pat's immediate reaction to the question will tell you whether or not it's true, no matter what he says."

"You really think so?" Peggy asked, looking more hopeful than when the conversation started.

"Yes, I ..."

A knock on the door interrupted Holly's reply.

"Can we come in?" Jasmine said through the closed door. "Violet's got something important to tell you."

32 SECRET SOCIETY

"What fresh hell is this?" Holly shook her head as she got up to open the door.

Ivy, Fern and the twins came in. Fern went directly to Peggy and sat down beside her. "How you doing?"

"Better." Peggy flashed a weak smile. "But what's this important news, Violet?"

"You're not gonna believe it." Jasmine grinned, went around the desk and dropped in the swivel chair.

"Well," Violet took a deep breath, "Before I got out of the van, I looked inside my bag for my phone and couldn't find it. When everyone else got out, I got down on the floor to see if it had dropped there. Just when I spotted it below the seat, I heard you tell Mr. Locksley to leave. He came up beside the van and that's when I heard him on his phone." Violet repeated the one-sided conversation she'd heard.

Holly threw her head back and groaned.

"I told you you weren't going to believe it." Jasmine smirked.

"There's a temple on the golf course?" Ivy's brow wrinkled.

"Oh, it's not really a temple," Peggy said. "The family of some past president donated a mausoleum-type structure in his memory. From time to time, they hold twilight cocktail parties out there as fundraisers — that sort of thing."

"Well, whatever it is, I think we should call the police," Ivy said.

"And tell them what?" Holly asked. "That there's going to be a bonfire of a secret society at the Country Club and that the incoming President of the Country Club is going to be appointed Supreme Commander? They'll just laugh at us."

"She's right," Jasmine said. "Besides, none of that is illegal, especially if it takes place on private property."

"But what if they do something awful?" Violet asked. "What if they perform an animal sacrifice? Or worse?"

"Whoa, Vy!" Jasmine held up her right arm, palm outward. "I know this secret society stuff is weird, but we have no reason to think something violent will take place. This is probably just a bunch of suburban dads dressing up in costumes, living out some goofball fantasy life. Fred Locksley is a tad obnoxious, but he doesn't impress me as a full-fledged psycho."

"But what about his wanting to be President of the Country Club? What if he murdered Hiram Thurston because he wasn't ready to retire and Locksley just didn't want to wait anymore?" Violet asked. "In my opinion, anybody with delusions of grandeur and salivating to be Supreme Commander of some secret society most definitely could be a murderer."

"What do you say, Peggy?" Fern asked. "You know him."

Peggy twisted her mouth from side to side as she considered the question. "I honestly don't know," she finally replied. "I'm sure you can tell I don't like Fred. He's just so — so…"

"Smarmy?" Holly offered.

Peggy grinned and nodded. "Yes, that's the perfect word."

"Is he married?" Ivy asked.

"Divorced," Peggy replied. "And he's relentlessly pursued every wealthy widow at the Country Club."

"Jeez, I can't imagine why no one snapped him right up," Jasmine scoffed.

"What about you, Peg?" Fern asked. "Why hasn't he pursued you?"

Peggy laughed. "Oh, he has. Actually Ron and Beverly tried to set us up. Ron thought he'd be the perfect husband for me. I made it clear I wasn't interested. Even my mother agreed with me, and that was the end of that."

"But what about now that your mother's gone?" Fern asked.

Peggy shrugged. "I didn't think of that. Maybe that's why he's been trying so hard to get to see me these last few days. Maybe he thinks that, with Mom gone, I'm once again 'in play'." She made air quotes around the words.

"Wait a minute," Holly said. "You're telling us that Ron likes this guy for you and even your mother didn't agree. Now, I'm with Violet. I'm very suspicious of him."

"What are you saying, Aunt Holly?" Jasmine asked. "You don't really think this guy could be dangerous, do you?"

Holly just shrugged.

"I'm with Holly on this," Fern said. "If Aunt Peg didn't like this guy, she had a good reason."

"Did your Mom ever tell you why she didn't like him?" Ivy asked.

Peggy shook her head. "All I remember is her saying 'best you stay away from him'."

"So where does that leave us?" Ivy asked, letting out a frustrated sigh.

Holly frowned. "If we can't go to the police, there's not

much more we can do."

"Not necessarily," Jasmine said, squinting.

"What are you suggesting?" Violet asked

Jasmine's mouth curled upward into a mischievous smile. "Anyone up for a moonlight ride?"

Holly scowled. "Absolutely not!"

33 SUPREME COMMANDER

"Okay, slow down," Fern said looking out the passenger side window of the van. "This is definitely the strip of road Tommy and I used to park on. Back then there was an unpaved service road that led to the Temple near the 9th hole of the golf course."

"Who knows if this service road still exists?" Holly muttered. "I can't believe I let you talk me into this."

"Oh, c'mon, Aunt Holly," Jasmine said from the second-row seat of the mini-van. "You know this is the only way we can find out whether Fred's just another kook or a maniacal killer." She tapped on the back of her mother's seat. "Now, what I still can't believe is that you and Dad used to sneak onto Country Club property late at night."

"Well, she ran away from home at 17. Sneaking a late night swim at the Country Club pool is light stuff compared to that," Holly scoffed as she slowed the car to a crawl along the dark stretch of road.

"Oh, just shut up, both of you. You need to be looking for a break in the trees." Fern lowered her window, cupped her eyes and peered out into the dark woods.

"Stop," Fern commanded. "There it is. They have kept the

service road here all these years."

"Should I drive down it?" Holly asked.

"No," Fern replied. "The trucks that used this made deep ruts. We always pulled over here and parked. Then we walked the rest of the way in."

Holly followed Fern's directions. As she turned off the ignition, her phone chirped. "That's probably Ivy checking on us." Holly pulled out her phone. "Oh no. Nick. I forgot to call him." She lifted the phone to her ear.

"Hi, Honey. I'm so sorry I forgot to call you. It's just been crazy here today. We solved the last riddle. Yeah, you're not going to believe this, but the treasure was an endangered plant that Peggy found growing in the backyard of our childhood home. Uh-huh. Yep. So we drove around Kingsdale and visited an old boyfriend of Peggy's and when we came back we started celebrating, and I can't believe it's after eleven. I know. I know. I'm sorry." Holly glanced at Fern and grimaced. "Yes, we'll be home tomorrow. I'll call you when we leave here. I love you more. Bye."

"You mean, you haven't told your husband what's been going on here? Fern asked.

"The detective?" Jasmine exclaimed in disbelief.

When Holly didn't reply, Fern prodded. "Do you lie to him all the time?"

Holly let out a long sigh. "Look, it's complicated. And I didn't lie."

Jasmine tilted her head to the side. "Oh yeah? What time you leaving tomorrow?"

Holly returned her niece's impish grin with a sour expression. She looked down at her phone. "It's 11:30. We need to go." Glancing back at Fern, she said, "You've got Jasmine's cell. If we're not back here by …"

"I know. I know," Fern said. "If you're not back in an hour,

I'll call the police and drive home."

"Ready?" Holly asked Jasmine as she silenced her phone.

"Ready," Jasmine said and slid open the side door.

Holly got out and walked to where Jasmine waited. Her niece looped her arm through Holly's and the pair started up the deeply rutted service road.

"Look at that moon," Jasmine whispered.

"*Bella luna* Nick would say," Holly replied as she looked upward. "I'm just glad it's so bright I don't need to turn on the phone light."

"I'd really like to meet Uncle Nick."

"Well, you have to come visit us in New Jersey. We're only ten miles from Manhattan. Have you been to New York?"

"No. After this is all over, we definitely have to make plans."

They continued in silence, making their way along the service road that sloped upward.

"Is it my imagination or does it look like there's a clearing up ahead?" Jasmine asked.

"I think you're right. Maybe it's the edge of the golf course." Holly sniffed. "Do you smell smoke?"

Jasmine inhaled. "Yeah. Maybe we need to get off this road and make our way through the trees before we reach the clearing."

"Unfortunately, I think you're right. Hope we don't disturb any wildlife creatures. Hold on to the back of my jacket," Holly said as she stepped off the road into the woods.

As they wove their way through the trees, the smell of smoke grew stronger. Suddenly, Jasmine bumped into Holly who had come to an abrupt stop. Ahead another ten yards the woods ended, and the landscape opened to a wide expanse.

"There," she whispered, pointing through the trees.

"Damn!" Jasmine said under her breath as she spotted the bonfire in front of a small building that resembled a temple. At least a dozen red-robed figures surrounded the blazing fire.

"Let's keep going until we reach the trees right at the edge of the clearing," Holly said.

Jasmine nodded and they continued slowly, careful not to make noise. As they drew closer to the opening, they heard chanting. Jasmine tugged on Holly's jacket sleeve.

"Maybe we shouldn't go any closer," she said.

Holly shook her head. "You've made me come this far. We're going to hear what they're saying."

Holly turned and continued in the direction of the bonfire. Jasmine gave her head a slight shake as she watched her aunt reach for a sapling and pull herself over a fallen tree. Nothing left to do but follow.

The further they went, the louder the chanting became. When they reached the last band of trees, Holly positioned herself behind the tree with the widest trunk. Jasmine came up behind her and they watched as at least a dozen robed figures paraded around the bonfire. At the sound of a clap, each lowered a torch into the fire until it ignited. Once the torches were lit, they lifted them skyward chanting unintelligible syllables as they did.

Suddenly the chanting stopped. A robed figure with a golden mask stepped onto the small porch of the Temple. The mask was difficult to make out from where they stood, but Holly thought it vaguely resembled Tony the Tiger, not a very ominous character.

"Brothers of the Blaze. Tonight we induct a new leader to the highest position of our order. That of Supreme Commander. We entrust him with our welfare and with leading and guiding us in making all our worldly decisions. Will our exalted leader please come forward."

Another robed figure, shorter than the first speaker, headed up the steps. The group gasped in unison when the exalted leader tripped on the step and tumbled forward.

Jasmine started to snicker. Struggling not to laugh herself, Holly quickly put her hand over her niece's mouth. When they looked back to the bonfire, two of the robed figures were helping the fallen one to his feet. The rest of the induction ceremony took place without mishap, culminating in the placing of a golden crown on the new Supreme Commander's head to the accompaniment of more chanting.

When the chanting ceased, Fred Locksley's voice boomed. "Brothers of the Blaze! I, your Supreme Commander, will not fail you. Under my tutelage, you will infiltrate the many unenlightened groups of which you are also members and bring them and their wealth into our fold. We will do what we must to conquer our foes and emerge victorious. Nothing — nothing will stop us."

34 NIGHTMARE

"And then ..." Jasmine burst into laughter. "And then, the exalted one tripped and landed spread-eagle on the steps. Oh, Mom, you should have seen it. You'd have wet your pants."

Holly giggled as she started the engine and pulled onto the road. Fern looked over at her. "My Jasmine has the sense of humor of a twelve year old boy. I want to know what you think. Did you find this all just silly nonsense?"

"Well, the tripping part was funny," Holly nodded before her expression quickly turned serious. "But Locksley's final words were a tad unnerving."

"What were they?" Fern asked.

"Oh, something about the members penetrating the groups they belong to and bringing them into the fold," Holly replied.

"Infiltrate is the word he used," Jasmine said. "And not just bring them in. He said bring them and their wealth into the fold."

"They're a cult," Fern said, "and like all cults, what they're really after is money."

Jasmine leaned forward. "That would definitely explain Fred's relentless pursuit of Peggy."

"And his wanting to be President of the Country Club." Holly flipped on her signal light and turned onto the main highway.

"Yeah, that would make a really sweet honey pot to 'infiltrate', wouldn't it?" Jasmine said.

"How big was the group?" Fern asked.

"Only about a dozen," Holly replied. "I suppose that's the good news."

"Yeah, and that must be the whole society," Jasmine added, "because I don't imagine anyone missing the induction of the Supreme Commander." Again, she let out a belly laugh.

"Do you think these men are dangerous?" Fern asked.

Holly sighed. "That's just it. They seemed a bit cartoonish, but Fred's final words — quite honestly, they gave me chills."

"And," Jasmine's tone grew suddenly serious, "I can't think of a better motive for murder. Getting Hiram Thurston out of the way makes it much easier to infiltrate the Country Club and accomplish their goal of gaining access to its members and their money."

No one said a word for the next few miles. As they neared the turnoff for the Lowe estate, Fern asked, "Do you think Ron's a member?"

"Oh, wow, Mom!" Jasmine exclaimed. "I didn't think of that."

"Wow is right," Holly nodded as she pulled onto the drive. "Peggy did say Ron thought Fred was a good match for her."

Fern nodded, "And if Aunt Peg knew about Fred — hell, if she even just heard rumors about him and his cult, that would explain her shutting down that whole plan."

Holly groaned. "This is a nightmare. Jasmine, is there any chance we can convince Jaworski to look into this?"

"I don't know, but I'm sure going to try. First thing tomorrow ..."

"Oh, my God!" Holly gasped as they approached the house. A police car with flashing lights sat directly in front of the Tudor mansion. Behind it, an ambulance idled, its lights also flashing.

Holly parked behind the empty ambulance, jumped out of the car and ran to the front door. The policeman who'd blocked her entry to the house the day they discovered Hiram Thurston's body in the library, again blocked the door.

"Get out of my way!" she said through gritted teeth.

Recognizing her, the officer stepped aside. Without waiting for Fern and Jasmine, Holly rushed inside. The main entry hall was empty, so she headed through the dining room to the kitchen.

"Oh, Holly," Ivy ran to her. "Thank God you're back."

Over her sister's shoulder, Holly saw Violet holding Peggy's hands as a member of the EMT crew talked to them. Higgins was busy arranging coffee mugs on the island as Mrs. Higgins plugged in the coffee urn.

"What happened?" Holly asked.

"Someone took a shot at Peggy when she stepped out onto her bedroom balcony."

Holly didn't reply. She pulled her phone from her pocket and tapped in a number.

"Hello, Nick ..."

35 MURDER INVESTIGATIONS — PLURAL

"What are you looking at?" Violet asked Jasmine as she entered the dining room and headed to the sideboard to check out the breakfast selection.

Without turning around, Jasmine waved her twin over to where she stood, peeking through the French doors out to the patio. "Come here."

Violet replaced the chafing dish cover she'd lifted and walked up beside her sister. "Who's that man?"

"Uncle Nick," Jasmine replied, grinning.

"No kidding?" Violet smiled back. "He's really good-looking."

"Yep, quite a hunk." Jasmine peered back through the window. "You know Aunt Holly didn't tell him anything about the murder and the rest of what's been going on here."

"You're joking? Why not?"

Jasmine shrugged. "All she told Mom and me was that it's complicated."

"Well, it sure looks like she's telling him everything now, doesn't it?" Violet said walking back over to the sideboard.

"Yep." Jasmine raised her chin in the direction of her aunt

and uncle. "And by the looks of it, he's not happy."

"Who's not happy?" Ivy entered the dining room and walked over to where Jasmine remained glued to the French doors.

"Uncle Nick," Jasmine replied as Ivy walked over and looked out to where Holly and Nick stood talking.

"Oh." Ivy backed away, her interest quickly diverted to the sideboard. "What smells so good?" she asked picking up a plate.

"Waffles," Violet replied as she sat down at the table. "Jasmine, stop gawking and come and get some breakfast."

After a moment, Jasmine backed away from the doors, picked up a plate and took the serving tongs from Ivy. "You don't seem concerned about what's going on out there."

"No," Ivy said as she filled a coffee cup and sat down across from Violet. "They'll work it out. They always do."

"Jasmine says Aunt Holly didn't tell Uncle Nick about the murder before last night." Violet gave Ivy a searching look. "Why wouldn't she?"

"Yeah," Jasmine said, taking a seat next to her sister. "Why wouldn't she?"

Ivy half-frowned, half-smiled. "Look, Nick's a cop. He doesn't exactly like it when we get involved in murder investigations."

"Wait. What?" Violet said, appearing confused.

Jasmine placed her hands flat on the table and leaned in. "Did you say '*when*' you get involved in murder investigations?"

Ivy lowered her head for a moment. When she looked back up, she burst into laughter. The identical twins wore identical expressions of disbelief, both wide-eyed and waiting for further explanation.

"Yes. That's actually how we met Nick. One of Holly's

neighbors was murdered when I came to visit her two years ago."

"But didn't you just say investigations, as in plural, as in more than one?" Jasmine asked.

Ivy pinched the bridge of her nose. "Yes. There may have been more than one."

"How many?" Violet asked.

Ivy looked up at the ceiling, "Well, counting Nick's cousin in Tuscany, four." She picked up her fork and stabbed a piece of waffle.

Violet and Jasmine stared at one another.

"I can't believe we're just hearing about this now." Jasmine shook her head.

"Finding out what?" Fern asked as she entered the dining room.

"Mom, did you know our aunts have been involved in murder investigations?" Violet asked.

"Four of them." Jasmine held up four fingers. "One in a foreign country."

"Really?" That explains why she didn't tell her husband about this one," Fern said as she walked over and started to fill a plate.

"Wait. You're not surprised?" Violet asked.

"Not really," Fern replied, taking a seat beside Ivy. "In case you two hadn't noticed, your aunts have been methodical in their approach to solving the riddle. And since we discovered the body in the library, they've been pretty matter-of-fact about everything."

Jasmine leaned back in her chair and crossed her arms. "You know, you're right." She glanced over at Ivy. "Most women your age would have had the vapors over a dead body in the house. I can't believe you two never mentioned any of this."

The half-frown, half-smile returned to Ivy's face. "It's not really something you bring up in polite conversation."

The French doors opened, and all eyes turned in that direction as Holly and Nick walked in.

"Oh good," Holly smiled. "You're all here. I'd like you to meet my husband, Nick. Nick, this is my sister, Fern, and these are her daughters, Violet and Jasmine. And, of course, you know Ivy."

"Hi, Nick," Ivy waved. "Glad to see you arrived safe and sound."

"Me too." Nick grinned and approached the table. Offering his hand to Fern, he said, "Nice to meet you."

"Likewise." Fern smiled back.

Nick backed up and put an arm around Holly, resting his hand on her shoulder. He looked at the twins and asked, "Remind me which one of you is Jasmine."

Jasmine raised her hand, wiggling her fingers. Her mischievous grin disappeared when Nick's expression turned stony.

"So, in spite of the fact that you're an Assistant DA, you talked my wife into going to a midnight crazy fest with a bunch of lunatics. You want to explain that to me, Counselor?"

36 MORE FRESH HELL

Holly poked Nick in the ribs. "That's not what I said, and you know it." She quickly turned to Jasmine. "He's kidding."

"He doesn't look like he's kidding." Jasmine appeared apprehensive as she stared back at Nick.

Holly poked Nick again, harder this time, and after a moment, the corners of Nick's mouth twitched. "What's for breakfast?" he asked as he glanced over at the sideboard.

"Come," Holly said, picking up a plate. As soon as her back was turned, Nick glanced back at Jasmine, pointing his index and middle finger at his eyes, then at hers, De Niro-style. Jasmine flashed him an amused smile in return as Violet giggled.

"Did anyone check in on Peggy this morning?" Holly asked as she sat down beside Fern.

"I did," Fern replied. "She's still a bit shaken, but she said she'd be down for breakfast as soon as she got dressed."

Jasmine gave Nick a wary, sidelong look as he took the seat next to her. "So, Uncle Nick, I hear you're a detective."

"Yep," he said, returning the sidelong glance. "And I have a badge and a gun." He speared a piece of sausage. "Now tell me about this Jaworski."

Just as Jasmine finished bringing Nick up-to-date on their

dealings with the local detective and her assessment of him, Peggy walked in.

"Good morning," she said, a weak smile on her face.

Nick immediately got to his feet and walked over to greet her. "I'm Nick," he said, taking her hand in his. "How you doing this morning?"

"I — I'm okay, but what about you? Did you get any sleep last night? You're here so early."

"Don't worry about me." Nick put his arm around Peggy and led her to the chair at the head of the table, closest to him. "Here. Sit down."

"I'll fix you a plate." Holly got up and went to the sideboard.

"Would you like orange juice?" Ivy asked as she stood up. "Coffee?"

"Oh, don't make such a fuss over me," Peggy protested.

"You just relax," Nick soothed. "You know there's no point arguing with the two of them?" He nodded in the direction of his wife and sister-in-law.

Peggy laughed. "Well, now I understand why Holly's been in such a hurry to get back home to you." She grinned as Holly handed her the breakfast plate. "You didn't say how handsome and charming your husband is, Holly."

Nick frowned and shook his head. "She doesn't like to brag."

Holly bowed her head, giving it a slow shake until the giggling in the room subsided. Nick kept his focus on Peggy. "So how many acres you have here?" he asked. "Coming up the drive, I felt like I was on the Ponderosa."

Peggy smiled and launched into a detailed description of the property. As everyone finished their breakfast, the conversation drifted from the size of the Lowe estate to local weather conditions and the Pocono Mountain tourist attractions. When Peggy finally put her fork down and drank the last of her coffee, Nick reached over, putting his hand on top of hers. "You feel up to talking to me about what happened last night?"

Peggy let out a small sigh. "It all happened so fast. I'm afraid there's not a lot I can tell you."

"Just tell me what you can remember," Nick said gently.

"Well, I went up to my room around ten." She frowned. "That's why I didn't even know Holly, Fern and Jasmine went out."

Nick just nodded.

"I fell asleep, but something woke me, so I got out of bed and went out on the balcony—I guess it was around 11:00. Lucky for me, a button from my robe came loose and I bent down to get it. That's when a shot shattered the flowerpot next to where I was standing. I screamed and dropped down. The next thing I knew Ivy and Violet were helping me inside."

"You said something woke you. Do you think it was a gunshot?" Nick asked.

"I suppose it could have been. I honestly don't know."

"Did you put a light on when you got out of bed?"

Peggy wrinkled her brow as she considered the question. "Yes, I did."

"You didn't see anything from the balcony. No movement?"

"No," Peggy shook her head.

"No flash of light?"

"Wait." Peggy closed her eyes for a moment "Yes. Right before I bent down to pick up the button, I did see a light. Just a quick flash of red, and then ..." She covered her face with her hands.

Nick squeezed Peggy's shoulder. "Hey, it's over. Your safe. We're not going to let anything happen to you."

"Excuse me, Miss Peggy," Higgins said from the doorway.

"What is it?" Peggy asked. The butler walked over and bent close to her ear. She shook her head, appearing even more distraught after he whispered something to her.

"What is it?" Holly asked.

"Ron is here," Peggy replied, "with Fred Locksley."

"More fresh hell." Jasmine snorted as she got to her feet. "Let me take care of this."

37 A PROPOSAL

"Don't worry," Fern said. "Jasmine will get rid of them."

"You don't want to see them?" Nick asked Peggy.

"No. I really ..." Peggy began, but the sound of shouting stopped her from finishing her sentence.

Ron burst into the room, shouting back over his shoulder at Jasmine who was directly behind him.

"You're the one who doesn't belong here!" he shouted. "You can't stop me from seeing my sister."

Nick got to his feet. "No, but I can."

His cheeks flushed, Ron appeared startled when he turned and faced Nick. For a moment, he seemed uncertain about what to do. But only for a moment.

"Who the hell are you?" he sneered.

"Nick Manelli."

"So?" Ron placed his hands on his hips in a pugnacious stance. "Who are you to keep me from seeing my sister?"

"Yes." Fred Locksley pushed past Jasmine and came up alongside Ron. "You're not a member of this family," he said jutting his chin forward.

Peggy slapped the table with both her hands and got to her

feet. "He's my cousin's husband and that's more family than you, Fred."

Jasmine smiled and returned to her place at the table as everyone in the room stared at Peggy for a moment, including Nick who put a supportive hand on her shoulder and gave it a gentle squeeze. She looked up at him, flashed a brief smile, then looked back at her brother.

"Ron, I already told you I'm not moving out of this house and you and Beverly are not moving in."

"That's not why I'm here," Ron said, his tone now less domineering. "I want — that is, Fred wants to talk to you."

"And exactly what could Fred possibly want to talk to me about?" Peggy said, her tone now combative.

"Could we ..." Fred bowed slightly, "could we talk in private?"

"No." Peggy said with force.

"Please, Peggy," Fred said. "This is a — a personal matter."

Peggy crossed her arms in front of her. "Fred, if you're here to propose marriage, I can assure you that I would not marry you if you were the last person on this earth."

Fred winced. "But Peggy," he whined, taking a step toward her. He stopped when Nick took a step forward.

"Get out!" Peggy said.

"Peggy, you're making a big mistake here," Ron said, his voice tight as he appeared to be struggling to control his temper. "You need to hear what Fred has to say."

"No, Ron, I don't, and I can't believe you're here on Fred's behalf. Since I was a teenager, you constantly cautioned me about men being interested in me just for my money. And here you are advancing this gold digger's case!"

"I'm no gold digger," Fred protested.

Peggy glared at him. "Seriously, Fred? Is there even one wealthy widow at the Country Club who you haven't tried to marry?" Peggy snorted. "For heaven's sake, you even courted Marion Bigsley who was fifteen years older than you and on oxygen. Luckily for her children she died before you even got to propose."

"That's a lie!" Fred held his hand to his chest, appearing deeply offended.

Peggy shook her head in disgust and turned her gaze back to Ron. "You are my brother and if you'd like to visit me, you're welcome here. But get this straight. I'm not leaving my home. You and Beverly are not moving in with me, and I am never, ever, ever marrying Fred Locksley."

Ron clenched and unclenched his fists as he stared back at his sister. His cheeks again grew ruddy as he appeared to be considering his next move.

"Excuse me," Higgins said as he entered the room and walked over to Peggy. Nick took a step back and made eye contact with Holly who shrugged and flashed him a grim smile.

The butler whispered something to Peggy. She sighed loudly and nodded, sitting back down. When Higgins disappeared back out into the hallway, Fred moved close to Ron and the pair spoke in hushed tones.

Ron pulled away from Fred when he saw the butler usher his son into the room. "Ronnie, what are you doing here?"

"Mom sent me," Ronnie replied, then turned to face his aunt. "I apologize for barging in like this, Aunt Peggy." Handing the flowers to her, he said, "These are for you. We heard about what happened last night. Glad to see you're okay."

"Last night?" Ron glared at his sister. "What the hell happened here last night?"

38 GOOD RIDDANCE

"What happened last night is nothing that concerns you," Peggy glared right back at her brother. Smiling at her nephew, she said, "Thank you, Ronnie. This is very thoughtful of you."

"I can't take credit," he said with an 'aw-shucks' expression. "They were Mom's idea."

"Well, thank her for ..."

"I asked you what happened here last night," Ron said, his reddened face looking very much like a volcano about to erupt.

"Well, you're going to find out anyway," Peggy said dropping down in her chair. "Someone took a shot at me on my balcony."

"What!" Ron screamed. "And you think you can manage here without a man? Let me tell you ..."

Ron charged across the room at his sister. Ronnie tried to stop him, but his father pushed right past him. Nick stepped between Peggy and her raging brother, grasped his wrist, and twisted his arm behind his back. Ron spewed obscenities into the air as Nick hustled him out of the room and down the hall.

"Sorry, Aunt Peggy." Ronnie frowned apologetically and quickly exited.

Fred Locksley stood frozen in place. Jasmine got up and

tapped him on the shoulder. "What are you waiting for, oh Supreme Commander? You're done here."

Fred's eyes widened, his mouth slightly open in an expression of horror. "Wha — what did you say?"

"You heard me. Vamoose!" Jasmine pointed to the door.

Fred's chin dipped downward as he scrambled out into the hall.

"Good riddance!" Jasmine scoffed as she stepped out into the hallway and watched to make sure he left through the front door.

"You okay, Peggy?" Fern asked reaching over and patting her cousin's hand.

Peggy laughed. "Okay is not quite the word I'd use."

Ivy got up and grabbed Peggy's coffee cup. "Well, you were magnificent," she said, refilling the cup.

"Yeah, you were even better than when you shut down Beverly the other day," Jasmine grinned.

Violet nodded. "Seriously, Aunt Peggy. I'm amazed at how you stood up to your brother. You didn't need any of us."

"Oh, but that's where you're wrong," Peggy demurred. "It's because I had you all around me that I had the nerve to tell my brother what I really felt."

"Don't underestimate yourself, Cousin. You have Donnelly blood running in your veins." Holly got up and headed to the door. "Let me go see what's keeping Nick."

Holly opened the front door, just in time to see Ronnie get in his car and drive off with his father in the passenger seat. Fred Locksley said something to Nick and then, head down, walked slowly to his car. It wasn't until Fred pulled out that she noticed another man standing beside Nick with his back to her. After a few moments, he turned around and Holly saw it was Detective Jaworski.

"Hello, Detective," she said when they reached the door. "I see you've met my husband."

"Morning," was Jaworski's terse reply.

Holly looked at Nick.

"The detective has some information on the case. He'd like to talk to your cousin. You think she's up to it?" Nick asked, his expression revealing nothing about the nature of the information.

"Yes, I think so," Holly replied. "Come in. Everyone's in the dining room," she said.

Jaworski stepped inside and headed across the main hall, not waiting for Holly or Nick.

Holly tugged on Nick's arm to stop him from following. "What's this about?" she whispered.

"He wouldn't say." Nick shrugged just as they saw Peggy, Jasmine and the detective exit the dining room and cross the hall in the direction of the office.

"Well, I guess we'll find out soon enough," Holly said.

Together they headed back to join the others in the dining room. They didn't have to wait long when they heard voices out in the hallway and the front door close. A few moments later, a somber-faced Jasmine appeared.

"They've arrested Pat Keefe for the murder of Hiram Thurston and the attempt on Peggy's life."

39 CONJECTURE

"Oh, no," Fern said. "How did Peggy take it?"

"Not well, I'm afraid." Jasmine sighed. "She tried to argue with Jaworski, but he said it was an open and shut case. The bullet from the gun that they pulled out of the flowerpot here matched the one that they removed from Hiram Thurston. They executed a search warrant and found the gun in Mr. Keefe's truck."

"Where is Peggy?" Holly asked.

"She ran upstairs before Jaworski even got out the door," Jasmine replied.

Fern got up. "I better go see how she's doing."

"I'll come with you," Violet said.

As they exited the room, Nick dropped down into a chair. "On what grounds did they get a search warrant?" he asked.

"He wouldn't tell me." Jasmine frowned.

"I don't care what evidence they have," Holly said. "I'm with Peggy on this. Pat would never hurt her."

"But he didn't, did he?" Nick leaned back in his chair.

"What are you saying?" Holly asked, her expression one of disbelief.

"Look. Your cousin is a very wealthy woman. Her brother may be an arrogant SOB, but he's not wrong about being suspicious of men who are interested in her."

"Oh, but they were childhood sweethearts," Ivy protested. "If you saw how he looks at her, you'd know Holly's right."

"You're missing the point. I'm not saying he doesn't care for her." Nick flashed his sister-in-law an indulgent smile. "But did you hear the last question Ron asked her?"

"You mean before you twisted his arm half-way up his back and hustled him out of here?" Jasmine smirked.

Nick ignored the comment, then answered his own question. "What he said was 'you think you can manage here without a man'."

"But what has that got to do with Pat?" Ivy asked.

"Some men try to manipulate women by creating situations to make them frightened," Nick replied. "Then they can step in and come to her rescue."

"You mean become her knight in shining armor?" Ivy's expression turned wistful.

Holly sat down. "I can see Ron and Fred doing that, but based on what I told you about Pat, what would make you suspect him of being that kind of man?"

"Whoever shot at Peggy, missed her. When I questioned her before, she said she remembered seeing a flash of red light. That means the gun was equipped with a laser sight. Unless you have no experience with a gun, it's pretty hard to miss your target."

"But she told you she bent down to pick up a button that came off her robe," Holly said.

"That's a possibility," Nick conceded. "But can you agree that it's also possible that whoever fired the gun cared about her and only meant to scare her?"

Holly twisted her mouth as she considered the question. "Yes,

I guess it's possible."

"Well, here's the million-dollar question," Jasmine said. "If it wasn't Pat, who was it? We know where Fred Locksley was last night."

Ivy got up to refill her coffee cup. "What about Ron?"

"I don't know." Jasmine shook her head. "He actually seemed blind-sided when his son said he was sorry about what happened last night."

"Yeah," Holly added. "And seeing how tight Fred and Ron are, Ron may have been one of those hooded figures at the induction ceremony last night."

"But couldn't Fred have put someone up to it and not told Ron?" Ivy asked.

"Yeah," Jasmine nodded. "I'm sure the Supreme Commander would have no trouble getting one of his minions to do his dirty work."

"Yes, that sounds like him," Holly agreed. "And having someone do it while he had an airtight alibi would be perfect."

"You're really stretching here," Nick said.

"But think about it, Nick," Holly said. "Fred had a motive to kill Hiram Thurston. He wanted to be President of the Country Club. So, he shoots Hiram and brings the body and dumps it in the library. That gets Hiram out of the way, and it's his first attempt to scare Peggy, so he can get his hands on the Lowe estate and fortune."

"Yeah," Ivy said, sitting back down beside her sister, "but it doesn't work the way he planned because we're all here. Remember, he kept coming around to try to talk to her."

"Right," Jasmine nodded. "So, when that didn't work, he comes up with a plan to scare her more up-close-and-personal, gets someone to fire a shot at her last night, and shows up here this morning to propose marriage and save her from the big, bad wolf."

"And he's got the perfect alibi for last night," Holly slapped the table.

"A nice theory," Nick added, "but it's total conjecture." He aimed a penetrating stare at Jasmine. "You know that, Counselor."

"I know," Jasmine nodded. "But I'm with them. I don't want it to be Pat Keefe."

"It was not Pat!" Everyone turned to see a tearful Peggy standing in the doorway. "And I'm counting on you all to prove it. Money is no object."

40 A PLAN

Jasmine got up and went over to Peggy. "Come on and sit down with us." She led Peggy to a seat at the table.

"I mean it," Peggy said, her expression steely. "I want you to find out who killed Hiram Thurston. Jaworski is so sure he has the guilty party, he's not going to investigate any further. Nick, can't you talk to him?"

Nick glanced down at his hands, then back up at Peggy. "I can, but I have to tell you police don't like outside interference, even if it is from another cop."

Peggy turned to Jasmine. "What about you? I'm clearly no longer a suspect in the case. You can represent Pat now. Then Jaworski would have to talk to you."

Jasmine made eye contact with Nick and smiled. "She's right." Turning her gaze back to Peggy she said, "Only one thing. I'm not licensed to practice in Pennsylvania."

"But can't you affiliate with a local firm?" Holly asked.

Peggy tapped the table excitedly. "Yes, yes. I'll call Charles. His firm deals mostly with wills and managing estates, but I'm sure he can assign a lawyer from his office to the case for this purpose."

"That could work." Jasmine nodded. "But I need to know

one thing. Are you in, Uncle Nick? I can't do this without a seasoned investigator."

All eyes turned to Nick, who looked over at Holly. "Do I really have a choice here?"

Peggy jumped up and threw her arms around his neck. "Oh, thank you, Nick."

"Hold on a second," he said as she let go. "I'll do this under one condition." He looked first at Ivy, then at Holly. "I'm in charge and nobody does anything without talking to me first."

Holly laughed and held up her right hand, extending her three middle fingers upward and folding her thumb across her palm over her little finger. "Scouts honor."

Ivy copied the gesture. "Me too."

"You're all too cute," Jasmine said shaking her head. "Now let's come up with a plan."

****

Two hours later Holly and Ivy stood at the front door watching as Nick, Peggy and Jasmine drove off.

"You think they'll be able to convince Jaworski to investigate Fred Locksley?" Ivy asked as she turned and walked back inside the house.

"If anyone can do it, Nick can," Holly said closing the door. "But you know he's right about cops not liking to be second-guessed. Remember Cyrus Bascom up in Reddington Manor?"

"Yes, but he was actually a criminal himself. Jaworski isn't Mr. Personality, but he didn't impress me as a dirty cop," Ivy said.

"Me either." Holly sighed as they headed to the patio. "This is the part I hate. Just waiting. I wish there was something we could do."

"Well, actually, there is one thing." Ivy waggled her eyebrows.

"What?" Holly narrowed her eyes askance.

"We could do our game of Clue."

Holly looked as if she'd just sucked a sour lemon.

"C'mon," Ivy coaxed. "I know it won't be the same without Kate, but what have we got to lose? I'll go to the office and see if I can find some pads and pens."

"All right. I suppose it will at least help pass the time." Holly picked a chaise lounge to drop down onto. As she did, Fern joined her on the patio.

"So," she said, sitting down on the wicker couch across from her younger sister, "tell me what you honestly think. Could Pat have done this?"

"Honestly?" Holly frowned. "I don't think so, but you never know."

"He seemed so genuinely at ease with himself and his life the day we visited and sat on his porch. Not edgy, like this Locksley character."

"I know it's hard to like Locksley, but that doesn't make him a murderer."

Ivy appeared in the doorway holding a stack of notepads and pens. "Look who I found in the library." She pointed her finger over her shoulder at Violet.

"What's all this?" Fern asked.

"Oh, Mom." Violet smiled as she plopped down on the couch beside her mother. "We're going to play a game of Clue."

"A what?" Fern asked.

Ivy handed her a pad and pen. "We each make four columns on our pads. Means, motive and opportunity."

"Then we list everyone who's a suspect and try to fill in the columns," Holly added.

Fern appeared amused. "You two do this often?"

"More than I'd like to admit," Holly said as she took the pad and pen her sister handed her.

"I think this is a great idea," Violet said, starting to draw lines for columns.

"Well, I'm putting Fred Locksley at the top of the list," Ivy said.

"Wait a minute." Fern held up her hand palm outward. "Are we talking about murdering Hiram or about trying to murder Peggy?"

"Good question," Holly said looking skyward. "I keep wanting to link the two, but you're right Fern. Maybe they're not related. Let's do one sheet for each separately."

"Well, Fred's at the top of my list for both," Ivy said.

"We may know his motive for killing Hiram Thurston, but why would he shoot at Peggy?" Violet asked.

"Oh, that's right," Ivy said. "You two weren't part of the conversation we had earlier with Nick and Jasmine." She went on to explain Nick's theory of men with a need to play hero/rescuer and Holly and Jasmine's theory on how Ron and Locksley may have worked together with an accomplice to pull off shooting at Peggy.

"Okay," Fern said as she finished writing. "So, I guess that same rescuer theory can apply to Pat."

"And remember a witness said they saw Hiram and Pat arguing the week before the murder," Holly added.

"I wonder what that was about," Violet said.

"Hopefully, Jasmine and Nick will find that out when they talk to him," Holly said.

"Okay." Ivy studied her pad. "So are these the only three suspects? I mean could someone we don't even know about have murdered Hiram?"

"And put the body in Peggy's library?" Fern said, her tone skeptical.

Ivy nodded. "You're right, Fern. Then it can only be one of these three men."

Holly squinted as she looked at her sister. "But maybe we're not looking at this the right way." She dropped her legs on either side of the chaise and sat forward. "We've sort of accepted Nick's theory, but what if someone really was trying to kill Peggy?"

"Oh, yes," Violet grimaced. "They could have put Hiram's body here to implicate her in his murder and when that didn't work, they tried to kill her."

"So, who benefits by getting Peggy out of the way?" Fern asked.

Before anyone could reply, Higgins appeared on the patio. "Ladies, Ms. Beverly Lowe would like to see you."

41 DONNELLY BLOOD

Peggy straightened her skirt and fidgeted in her chair as she sat staring through the plexiglass, waiting for Pat Keefe to be brought in. She caught her breath when he appeared, his face taut as he sat down facing her and lifted the phone.

Peggy just stared until Pat motioned for her to pick up the phone hanging on the wall. Her hands trembled as she fumbled with it. When she finally held the phone to her ear, she didn't know what to say and just stared mournfully at the man she once loved, and maybe still did.

"Peg, you didn't need to come," Pat said.

She continued to stare at him, appearing unable to speak, but after a few moments, she cleared her throat and asked, "Patrick Keefe, did you kill Hiram Thurston?"

Pat looked as if he'd been slapped in the face. "No."

"And did you take a shot at me on my balcony last night?"

"My God, Peggy, you know I would never do anything to hurt you." Pat appeared wounded by the question.

Peggy sat up straight, a determined look on her face. "Okay, then. My niece, Jasmine Brennan, is going to represent you, and Nick Manelli, my cousin's husband, is going to assist her in finding whoever is guilty and framing you for these crimes."

"Peg, I can't afford ..."

As he spoke, Peggy hung up the phone and got to her feet. At the door, she paused, then turned around picking up the phone again.

"One last question." She took a deep breath. "Did you take money from my stepfather to stay away from me?"

Pat stared back at her, his expression disconsolate. "No." Peggy, I would never ..."

Peggy dropped the phone and left the room.

****

"Hi, Pat." Jasmine said, extending her hand. "Sorry to be meeting you again under these circumstances. This is Nick Manelli, a detective in the homicide division of Pineland Park, NJ."

After shaking both their hands, Pat sat down and began, "Look, I know Peggy told me you'd be representing me, but I don't have the money to pay you."

"That's been taken care of." Jasmine dropped into a chair and rooted around in her bag for a pen.

"But I can't let Peggy ..."

"Listen, Pal," Nick intervened. "Peggy Lowe is my wife's cousin. They're Donnellys. Trust me. There's no "letting" or "not letting" a Donnelly woman do anything. She told us to clear your name and money is no object. So that's what we're gonna do. You just sit back and answer our questions. We'll do the rest."

Jasmine looked across the table, her pen poised to take notes. "Now, tell us about the argument you had with Hiram Thurston," she said.

Pat sat silently, staring at the table. After a few moments, he began. "For the last five years, I've been doing odd jobs out at the Country Club — handyman stuff — repairing lawn mowers, fixing leaking faucets — that sort of thing. Three weeks ago, Hiram called me in and said he was sorry, but they wouldn't have any more work for me. When I asked why, he told me there was a complaint about some of the jobs I'd done."

"And you got angry and that's when you got into an argument?" Jasmine prompted.

"Well, not at first. I asked him what the complaints were and who made them, but Hiram said he wasn't 'at liberty' to discuss it with me. That's when I got kind of heated." Pat looked from Jasmine to Nick. "I mean, after all these years I felt I deserved better than that. I deserved the right to defend my work, but how could I do that if he wouldn't even tell me what I did wrong?"

"And was Mr. Thurston equally heated?" Jasmine asked.

Pat shook his head. "No. It was weird. It was as if he felt sorry about having to let me go — maybe a little guilty even."

"You have any idea who might have been behind the complaints?" Nick asked.

"That's just it," Pat replied. "I talked to everyone from the landscaper to the building manager. Nobody I did work for in the last month said they complained about my work. In fact, they assured me they would have come to me first. Pete Smith, a friend of mine who works in the kitchen, did tell me there was a lot of strange stuff going on, a lot of infighting among the Board members. He said a lot of the guys were worried that Hiram was being forced out and whoever took over would fire everyone and bring in their own people."

"Any suggestions as to who was planning to take over?" Jasmine asked.

Pat shrugged. "He didn't say."

Jasmine nodded and flipped to a new sheet of paper on her legal pad. "The day Hiram Thurston's body was found in the library at the Lowe estate, you visited the estate. Why?"

"To see Peggy."

"Did it have anything to do with your being let go at the Country Club?"

Pat's brow furrowed. "No. Why would it?"

"The Lowes are well-connected at the Country Club. Did you think she might be able to help you get your job back?"

"No. That's not why I went to see her."

Jasmine looked across the table and pinned Pat with a penetrating stare. "Then why did you want to see her?"

Pat shifted in his chair. "It was a personal matter."

"Of a romantic nature?" Jasmine asked.

Pat appeared increasingly uncomfortable under Jasmine's piercing gaze. He sighed and finally answered her. "You know it was. Weren't you the one who teased us the day you all dropped by?"

"Maybe we should move on to another line of questioning," Nick said.

"You think the prosecution will do that?" Jasmine turned a withering glance in Nick's direction. "If I were the prosecutor, I'd say this man got fired by his employer and spurned by an old lover. Too much to handle, he snapped, murdered the employer and then tried to pin it on the woman as payback for her rejecting him. If he pussyfoots around the romantic issue like he just did, it will look like he's dodging the subject."

"She's right," Nick said to Pat.

"Okay. I saw Peggy after her mother's memorial service but couldn't get a moment alone with her. I hoped that if I dropped by the house, I might get a chance to talk to her privately, but the butler said she was out for the day, so I left."

"Where'd you go?" Nick asked.

"I went home."

Jasmine flipped another page on her pad. "Can anyone verify that?"

"I don't know. I live alone," Pat said. "Mrs. Zaruta, the lady next door, might have seen me. She's usually home all day."

"What about last night?" Nick asked.

Pat frowned. "Again, I was home by myself last night."

"How do you think the murder weapon got in your truck?" Jasmine asked.

Pat appeared genuinely distraught. "I don't know. You were to my place. I don't have a driveway. I park on the street. Anyone could have dropped that gun in there."

Jasmine exchanged a quick glance with Nick. "You have any other questions?" When Nick shook his head, she looked across at Pat. "That's all for now then. If you think of anything that might help us, here's my card with my cell number."

Pat took the card. "I know all together this looks bad for me. Tell me what you really think. Can you really mount a credible defense with this evidence against me and no alibi?"

"Yeah, it looks pretty bad," Jasmine flashed her droll smile. "But you've got something very important going for you. I've got Donnelly blood running through my veins too."

42 ANOTHER VISIT FROM BEVERLY

"Tell her we don't want to see her," Fern said to Higgins, making a shooing motion with her hands.

"No, wait, Higgins," Holly turned to Fern and in a hushed tone, said, "If anyone benefits from getting Peggy out of the way, it's Beverly. I think we should talk to her."

Fern shook her head. "Well, you can, but count me out."

"Higgins, would you please have Beverly wait for me in the drawing room," Holly said.

Ivy got up, dropping her pad and pen on the chair. "I'll join you."

"Good," Holly nodded as she got up.

"I'll stay with my mom," Violet said. "Maybe we can come up with something to add to this clue list."

****

"Hello, Beverly," Holly said as she entered the drawing room.

"What a lovely dress you have on." Ivy smiled. "I love that shade of pink."

Beverly gave Ivy an assessing once-over. She appeared uncertain, as if she couldn't believe Ivy was actually complimenting her. But after a moment, she smiled back and said, "Why thank you."

"Sorry, Peggy's not here." Holly sat down on the couch across from Beverly. "Is there something you'd like us to tell her when she gets back?"

"Well, I'm just feeling awful about how things have gone between us since the memorial service." Beverly's eyes darted from Holly to Ivy, coming to rest on her perfectly manicured hands resting in her lap.

"Yes, well after a death in a family, there can be a shift in the — uh — the family dynamic," Holly replied.

Again, Beverly appeared unsure of how to take the comment and sat staring at Holly.

Ivy filled in the uncomfortable silence. "Yes, we should know. Being sisters, we've attended our share of family funerals and have seen some of our family members just drift apart after a death. It's very sad. Do you have sisters, Beverly?"

"I do," Beverly said, looking much more comfortable now that the conversation had shifted to a safe topic.

As Ivy and Beverly engaged in small talk, Holly sat observing. She wondered when Beverly was going to get to the point of this visit. It didn't take too much longer.

"Well, I'm just glad this Keefe fellow is behind bars. I know Ron and I will sleep better knowing Peggy is safe. And to think he actually worked at the Country Club."

"You know, Peggy doesn't think Pat Keefe is guilty," Holly said.

"She doesn't?" Beverly placed her hand on her chest.

"No, she doesn't," Holly replied feeling there was something disingenuous about Beverly's reaction.

"Well, if it wasn't him," Beverly batted her eyelashes, "who does she think killed Hiram?"

"Oh, I don't think Peggy has any other suspects in mind," Ivy replied. "She's just positive it couldn't be Pat."

"You're pretty connected at the Country Club," Holly said. "Do you have any idea who might have wanted Hiram out of the way?"

"Out of the way? That's a funny way of putting it," Beverly replied.

"Well, what Holly means is that Hiram was an important man," Ivy intervened. "Important men often make enemies just because they have to make tough decisions that impact other people — people who may be negatively affected by those decisions."

Holly watched as Beverly considered Ivy's interpretation. After a moment, she said, "You know, you're right." She leaned in Ivy's direction, conspiratorial-like. "I'm not one to tell tales outside of school, but I did hear ..." Suddenly she stopped. "No, I shouldn't say anything."

"Certainly you can trust us," Ivy assured her.

Beverly hesitated only a moment before she continued. "Well, I heard there were some financial — shall we say — irregularities with the club's finances."

"What kind of irregularities?" Holly asked.

Beverly cast a calculated look at Holly. "Oh goodness. I'm sorry. I've already said too much." She jumped to her feet. "I really shouldn't take up any more of your time."

As Ivy started to get up, Beverly waved her hand. "No, no. You sit. I can see myself out." As she opened the door, she stopped. "Give my love to Peggy," she said and was gone.

Ivy turned to Holly. "Darn! Just when she was about to tell us something."

Holly shook her head and smiled. "I think she told us *exactly* what she wanted us to know."

43 THE NEIGHBORS

"Have a seat." A tired-looking Detective Jaworski pointed to the chairs in front of his desk. "Let me guess. You don't think Pat Keefe killed Hiram Thurston."

"Your assistant went over the evidence with us earlier," Jasmine replied. "We understand your case. But we think Mr. Keefe is being framed."

Jaworski's eyebrows shot upward. "Golly, I never heard that one before." His gaze turned to Nick. "That a new one for you, Detective Manelli?"

"No sir," Nick replied. "I have heard that many times. But Mr. Keefe parks his truck on the street, and anyone could have put that gun in it. Were his prints found on the gun?"

"We don't have the results from forensics yet, but so what? If his prints weren't on the gun, he could have just wiped it clean." Jaworski said wearily.

"And then left it in the back of his truck?" Jasmine asked.

"Don't know about you two, but in my experience, criminals aren't all that bright."

"Were the neighbors questioned?" Nick asked.

"We didn't need to question them. We had the murder weapon." Jaworski jutted his jaw forward. "You questioning how

I do my job?"

"No sir," Nick replied. "I was just wondering if anyone in the neighborhood saw something — like a stranger on the street maybe."

Jaworski appeared to relax a bit. "Look, you want to talk to the neighbors, go ahead. Now, if you'll excuse me." Jaworski picked up a pen and looked down at the papers on his desk. "I have work to do."

Nick nodded to Jasmine and got up. "Thank you for your time, Detective."

Jaworski didn't look up as they left the office. When they reached the lobby, Jasmine's phone pinged.

"It's Aunt Peggy. She says Higgins picked her up and they're on their way home."

"Good," Nick said holding the door open. "Do you know how to get to Pat Keefe's house?"

"Yeah," Jasmine replied. "I guess we're going to talk to the neighbors."

"You guessed right."

****

A blood-curdling bark sounded as Nick and Jasmine started up the steps of the house next door to Pat's. The barking grew more fierce as Nick knocked on the door.

"Hush, Sparky," a woman said as she came to the door. The dog's bark transformed to a low growl.

"Mrs. Zaruta, I'm Jasmine Brennan and this is …"

"Brennan?" The woman squinted through the screen. Her hair was snow white, woven into a thick braid that encircled the top of her head. She wore a farmers' market apron, and the aroma of something baking wafted through the screen door. "Are you John Brennan's daughter?" she asked.

"No, Ma'am. I'm actually Tom Brennan's daughter."

"Tom Brennan." The woman repeated the name and pursed her lips. "You mean Tommy Brennan who moved to Florida, gosh, has to be about thirty or more years ago?"

"Yes, Ma'am. That Tommy Brennan."

The older woman broke into a smile. "How is little Tommy? People said he was a wild one, but I always liked that boy. If he saw me walking back from the store, he always offered to carry my grocery bag."

"Unfortunately, my father passed away," Jasmine replied.

Mrs. Zaruta's smile quickly morphed into a sorrowful expression. "Oh, I'm so sorry to hear that." She shook her head.

"Mrs. Zaruta …"

"Say, didn't he marry Fern Donnelly?"

"Yes, Fern Donnelly is my mother."

"And is your Mom still with us?"

"Yes. Yes, she is, but Mrs. Zaruta, I'm here because I'm a lawyer and I'm representing Pat Keefe."

"Pat! Oh my goodness. I don't care what anyone says, that boy is no murderer."

"Well, we're happy to hear you say that because we don't think so either and we're hoping maybe you can help Pat by answering a few questions."

"Heavens, yes. I'd do anything to help Pat. Why if it wasn't for him …" Mrs. Zaruta stopped, glancing over at Nick as if she just noticed he was standing there. "And who's this handsome fella with you?"

"This is Detective Nick Manelli."

"Detective?" the old woman said smiling.

"Yes," Jasmine nodded. "He's Holly Donnelly's husband."

"Holly! Oh my!" Mrs. Zaruta peered through the door past Nick and Jasmine. Is she here with you? She went to school with my John." Her brow wrinkled. "Or was it my Billy?"

"Ma'am, do you think we could come inside? We won't be long." Nick said.

"Goodness yes! Where are my manners? Sparky, you go lie down," she said as she unlatched the screen door and opened it. "Come in. Please sit down in there." Mrs. Zaruta, pointed to the living room. "Let me go check on my lemon pound cake. I'll get us some iced tea while I'm at it," she said, heading to the kitchen. "And don't you worry about time. You can take as long as you like."

Sitting down, Jasmine exchanged a glance with Nick and snickered. "You didn't have any other plans for the afternoon, did you?"

44 CATCH UP

It was six o'clock when Nick and Jasmine returned to the Lowe Estate. Holly was waiting out front. When Nick got out of the car, she put her arms around him.

"I thought you were never going to get here," she said giving him a hug.

As Nick kissed her, Jasmine snickered. "Hey, you two! Get a room."

Holly cast a disparaging glance at her niece. "Excuse us, but we haven't seen each other in a while."

"What? All of four days?" Jasmine mocked.

"Speaking of room," Nick said, "let me go get my overnight bag out of the car."

"No need," Holly smiled. "Higgins got it and already put it in the room Mrs. Higgins prepared for us."

Jasmine laughed at Nick's slightly incredulous expression. "You're gonna love it here, Uncle Nick," she said, leading the way inside.

"Everybody's in the dining room," Holly said as they entered the main hall. "Are you two hungry?"

"Starved," Jasmine replied.

"I could eat," Nick said.

Peggy looked relieved as the threesome entered the dining room. "Come sit by me," she said, aiming the invitation at Nick. "Higgins, would you bring a plate for Nick and Jasmine, please."

"Certainly," the butler replied and headed to the kitchen.

"What took you so long?" Fern asked.

"Mrs. Zaruta." Jasmine raised both eyebrows.

"Oh, I remember the Zarutas," Ivy said. "I went to school with their daughter Mary Ellen."

"Yeah, John Zaruta was in my class," Holly added.

"Sure it wasn't Billy?" Jasmine asked, smiling.

Peggy waved her hand impatiently. "All I want to know is did you learn anything that can help clear Pat?" Peggy asked.

Nick nodded. "We did."

"It took forever for us to get it out of her, but the old lady can definitely provide an alibi for the shooting last night," Jasmine said. "She saw Pat through the window at eleven when she took her dog out. That clears him of taking a shot at Peggy."

"Thank you," Nick said as Higgins placed a plate loaded with roast beef, mashed potatoes smothered in gravy and a whopping helping of vegetable medley. As Higgins made his way around the table to Jasmine, Nick continued. "The really good news is that Mrs. Zaruta will testify that her dog woke her up barking at about three A.M. She looked out the window and saw a man standing near Pat's truck. She shouted out the window at him and he took off."

"Like a bat out of hell, she said." Jasmine admired the plate of food Higgins placed in front of her and dug into the mashed potatoes.

"But did she see him drop the gun in Pat's truck?" Ivy asked.

Jasmine shook her head, her mouth too full to answer.

"No," Nick replied. "She didn't recognize him either."

"But this woman's testimony would raise doubts in the minds of the jury, wouldn't it, Jaz?" Violet asked her sister.

Jasmine swallowed. "Absolutely."

"Did you tell Jaworski all of this?" Peggy asked.

Nick frowned. "He wasn't in when we stopped back at the office, but we filed a report with the desk officer."

Her expression somber, Peggy nodded slightly. "This is all good."

"And *we* have something to tell you," Ivy smiled at Nick and relayed the conversation they had with Beverly.

"So, you think she wants us to look into these financial irregularities at the Country Club?" Nick asked.

"Yes," Holly replied. "She acted all flustered, like she spilled the beans, but it definitely was a well-rehearsed performance."

Jasmine turned to Peggy. "Financial irregularities at a private organization aren't usually anything members care to talk about. Aunt Peggy, do you know anyone at the Country Club who would even consider talking to us?"

Peggy bit her lip. "I've been thinking about whether or not to tell you this …"

Nick reached over and put his hand on top of hers, giving her his laser beam stare. "The best way for you to help Pat is for you to tell us whatever you know, Peggy."

A tear rolled down her cheek. "Ron is the Board Treasurer."

"What?" Holly exclaimed. "And his wife tips us off that there may be financial irregularities at the club?"

Fern let out a scornful laugh. "What did I tell you about that bi … that witch? She'd turn in her own grandmother if it served her purpose."

"But what's her purpose?" Ivy asked, her expression one of bewilderment. "Exposing her husband to criminal charges?"

Fern snorted. "If I were married to that cretin, sorry, Peggy, but short of murder, I couldn't think of a better way to get rid of him."

Jasmine lowered her fork to her plate. "But what if it's the opposite? What if she's heard the rumors about financial malfeasance and is worried her husband's in jeopardy? If it is, so is her standing in the community."

"Yeah," Nick nodded. "She may want us to investigate and clear her husband."

"Oh boy!" Holly said under her breath. "Like we don't have enough on our plates."

"Do you feel like you can talk to your brother about this?" Nick asked Peggy, his tone gentle.

"I can't," she replied. "I know my brother. No matter what I said, he'd think I was accusing him of a crime and fly off the handle." She shook her head. "No. I just can't."

"Okay, I get that," Jasmine said. "But surely there's someone else you know at the Country Club who you can talk to."

Peggy's doleful expression transformed into a frown. "That's just it. I've been thinking about nothing else since Holly told me about Beverly's visit. With Hiram gone, I'm not sure who I could talk to. I know all of the Board members, but not well enough for them to confide in me. Besides wouldn't they wonder why I came to them and not to my own brother?"

"You're right," Nick agreed. "But what about one of the workers? Pat said a guy from the kitchen told him there was a lot of infighting going on among the Board members."

"Hey, what about that young woman who came to get Hiram when he was talking to us after the memorial service?" Holly asked.

"Yeah." Ivy nodded. "The greeter."

"That's the one." Holly looked at Peggy. "I'll bet she can tell us something."

"Why didn't I think of her?" Peggy said, excitement in her voice. "That's Georgette's cousin, Cassie Snyder ."

"Who's Georgette?" Nick asked.

"My sister-in-law, Don's wife. They're on a cruise." Peggy tapped the table with her fist. "Darn! I don't know Cassie all that well. It would be so much better if we could ask Georgette to talk to her. You sure we can't wait until she and Don get back?"

"We really don't have time to waste," Jasmine said. "Look, it's not like you're a stranger. You're an important member of the Club. I'm sure she'll speak to you."

"I guess you're right," Peggy said, not looking entirely convinced.

"Clearly she worked closely with Hiram," Ivy said. "Was she his assistant?"

Peggy nodded.

"That means she'd know that Hiram trusted you." Holly said, turning to Nick. "What do you think?"

Nick put his knife down and looked from Holly to Peggy. "They're right. Pat told us the workers were afraid that they were all going to lose their jobs. This young woman might be eager to talk to someone who could be in a position to help her."

Peggy tapped the table with both hands. "Okay, then. I'll talk to her."

****

Holly hung her slacks in the closet and gave an admiring glance around the room she and Nick had been moved into. She walked over to the window and peeked through the curtains at the vast expanse of the front lawn, visible due to some exquisite lighting design. Even after dark, they had quite a view.

The bathroom door opened to a view she enjoyed even more. A bare-chested Nick stepped out. "Have I missed you," she said, walking over to him, her arms outstretched.

"Not so fast," he said, grasping her wrists. "You know I'm still annoyed that you didn't tell me what was going on here until you had no other choice."

Holly grimaced. "I — I'm sorry."

"How sorry?"

Holly flashed a coquettish grin. "Can we get in bed to finish this discussion?"

"You're lucky I love you," he said, pulling back the covers.

45 CASSIE

Peggy pulled her Audi into a parking space near the front entrance to the Country Club.

"You ready?" Holly asked.

"I am," Peggy replied, a tone of resignation in her voice. "Thanks for agreeing to come with me. Don't take this the wrong way, but I'd feel a lot better if Georgette were with me."

"Yeah, me too," said Holly, "but I'm sure you can handle this. Just remember the things we rehearsed. If you get stuck, I'll ask a question or make a comment to keep you on track."

Inside, the lobby was deserted. "This way," Peggy said crossing to a corridor on the other side of the entrance hall. They passed two closed doors, arriving at a third which was slightly ajar. Peggy gave it a light tap and peered inside.

"Cassie."

The young woman who had been focused on a computer screen looked up at Peggy. "Oh, Ms. Lowe. Good morning." She smiled. "I received your check in the mail yesterday. Thanks for paying so promptly."

"Of course," Peggy smiled back. "I pride myself on never having paid a bill late in my entire life."

"I'll bet not many people can say that." Cassie laughed.

185

"What brings you here today?"

"I was wondering if you had a moment to talk to us." Peggy looped her arm through Holly's. "This is my cousin Holly Donnelly."

"Yes, I remember meeting you the day of the memorial service," the young woman said. "Please. Sit down." She pointed to the chairs in front of her desk. Once they were seated, she asked, "So what can I do for you?

Peggy inhaled deeply and began. "You know that the police have arrested Pat Keefe for Hiram's murder."

The smile faded from the young woman's face. "I know Pat. He's done a lot of work here over the years — such a nice man. I find it hard to believe he killed Mr. Thurston. But why do you want to talk to me about it?"

"I know you were Hiram's trusted assistant. I don't know how many times he told me and Mother, he'd be lost without you." Peggy smiled.

Cassie's eyes filled up. "He was very good to me."

"I don't believe for one minute that Pat is guilty. I'm here to talk to you about a sensitive Board matter that may relate to Hiram's murder." Peggy moved forward in her chair, grasping the front edges of Cassie's desk. "Would you like to help us find his murderer?" she asked.

"Of course, but I don't see how I can help." Cassie shifted nervously in her chair.

"I'll come right to the point. We heard a rumor that there may be some irregularities with the Country Club finances and we think that may have something to do with Hiram's murder."

The color drained from Cassie's face. "I — I don't think I can ..." She looked past Peggy and Holly to the open door.

Holly quickly got up, closed the door and returned to her seat.

"I know I'm asking a lot here," Peggy said, "but I promise you that whatever you tell us, we will keep confidential and never let anyone know you spoke to us. Cassie, whatever you tell us could free an innocent man and help bring Hiram's killer to justice."

Holly and Peggy waited silently as Cassie lowered her head, appearing to struggle with how to reply. After a few moments, she looked up at Peggy. "All right. For Mr. Thurston's sake, I'll tell you ..."

The door behind them opened. "Cassie! Didn't I tell you ..." An irate Fred Locksley stopped in the doorway. When he saw Peggy, his angry expression morphed into his signature smarmy smile. "Peggy, what a pleasant surprise." He glared across the desk at Cassie, his expression once again transforming, this time into one of annoyance. "Why didn't you let me know Ms. Lowe was here?"

"Fred, I came to see Cassie, not you. That's why," Peggy said not trying to hide her irritation at his interruption.

"But Peggy, dear," Fred's obsequious posture returning, "anything concerning the Club concerns me, especially for a member of your stature."

"Oh, please," Peggy scoffed.

"Now, now, Peg," he soothed. "Why don't you come into my office and tell me what this is all about."

"Because this is about a homecoming party for my brother Don and his wife Georgette at my house and has nothing to do with the club," Peggy sneered. "You do know that Cassie and my sister-in-law Georgette are cousins, don't you, Fred?"

"No, I didn't know that," Fred admitted, staring at Cassie as if he'd never really seen her before.

Standing up, Peggy said, "Let's go, Holly. Cassie, give me a call tonight or drop by the house to help me finish making plans." She turned to face Fred. "If you want to be a president as well regarded as Hiram Thurston, I suggest you get to know the people who work for you," she sneered. "And just so you know, you're not invited to the party. Cassie is."

46 SURPRISES

"Oooh! I could just scream!" Peggy said as she hit the start button.

"Calm down," Holly said, fastening her seatbelt.

"Damn that idiot!" Peggy backed out of the parking space. "Just when Cassie was about to tell us something." She pounded the steering wheel with her fist, then gunned the engine, skidding across the lot and onto the exit road.

"Peggy, slow down," Holly urged. "Getting us into an accident will not help the situation."

Peggy took a deep breath. "You're right. I'm just so angry."

"Don't be." Holly chortled. "Once again, you were magnificent."

"I was?" Peggy's brow wrinkled.

"You were. Your cover story for why we were there talking to Cassie couldn't have been better. And you didn't hesitate a second. How did you come up with it so fast?"

Peggy smiled, clearly enjoying her cousin's praise. "I actually had been thinking about having a small get-together when Don and Georgette get back home, so it just sort of came to me."

Holly nestled back in her seat. "Well, it was a perfectly

plausible reason for us to be there. Better yet, I think you secured Cassie's position for life. Mr. Locksley will not look at her the same way now that he knows she's related to the Lowe family."

Turning onto the highway, Peggy sighed. "But what do we do now?"

"Wait for Cassie to call."

"But what if she doesn't? She was so reluctant to tell us anything at first. What if she was so freaked out by Fred's bursting in on her that she decides she doesn't want to risk losing her job by telling us what she knows?"

"She'll call," Holly said with more conviction than she felt. If she were Cassie, she'd be worried about losing more than her job.

****

As the mansion came into view, Holly noticed the minivan parked in front. "I don't believe it. Nick and Jasmine must be back already."

"Do you think that means good news or bad news?" Peggy asked.

"Only one way to find out," Holly said, unbuckling her seat belt as Peggy brought the car to a stop.

Inside they paused a moment when they heard laughter.

"Sounds like good news to me." Holly smiled and headed across the entry hall in the direction of the merriment. When they found the dining room vacant, they continued through the French doors to the patio. Jasmine was pouring champagne into crystal flutes that Violet and Ivy were passing around.

"Perfect," Jasmine said when she spotted them near the doorway. "You're just in time for the toast."

Ivy handed a flute to Peggy. "Oh, you're going to be so happy." She took Peggy by the arm and guided her over to the seating area.

Peggy stopped and caught her breath when she saw a smiling Pat Keefe seated between Fern and Nick on the wicker couch. Nick immediately got up and made room for her. Pat scrambled to his feet.

"Peg, I don't know how to thank you," he said, taking both her hands in his.

"Oh, I think it's Nick and Jasmine you need to thank." Peggy flushed scarlet and looked down at her feet.

"Oh, sit down, you two," Fern said taking a flute from Violet. "Who's going to make the toast?"

"I will," Jasmine said lifting her glass. "To truth, justice and the American way."

Everyone laughed before sipping their champagne.

"I hope you don't mind," Jasmine said to Peggy. "The only bubbly I could find was this Dom Perignon. You weren't saving it for something special, were you?"

Peggy grinned shyly. "If I was, I'd say this counts as something special."

"Okay, so tell us everything," Holly said. "How did you spring Pat?"

"My expert legal arguments, how else?" Jasmine said.

Nick shook his head. "Don't listen to her. We hadn't even finished telling Jaworski about Mrs. Zaruta when the forensic and ballistics test results came in. "There was no gunshot residue on Pat's skin or clothing, and there were fingerprints on the gun, but they weren't Pat's."

"Who's were they?" Ivy asked.

"They didn't match anything in the system," Nick replied.

"So the test results plus Mrs. Zaruta's statement were all they needed to release Pat," Jasmine added, again raising her glass in a celebratory salute.

Peggy smiled, but the smile disappeared as her gaze came to rest on Nick. "Was the gun registered? Do they know who it belonged to?"

Nick nodded.

"Tell me," Peggy said. "Who?"

Nick grimaced. "The gun is registered to Ron Lowe."

47 THE LAST OF THE CHAMPAGNE

Peggy lowered her champagne flute to the table. "That can't be." She shook her head. "Excuse me," she muttered as she got up and ran through the French doors back into the house.

Fern drained the last of the champagne in her glass. "I'll go," she said, getting up and following her.

"Me too." Violet stood up, held her glass for Jasmine to re-fill and followed her mother.

"Way to go, Uncle Nick." Jasmine sank down on the love-seat. "You sure know how to clear a room." She glanced over at Holly. "Is he always this much of a buzz kill?"

"Did you want me to lie to her?" Nick asked, dropping into the spot Peggy had vacated.

"He's right," Ivy said. "She had to know the truth."

"Damn!" Pat said under his breath.

"Sorry, this put a damper on your celebration," Ivy said.

"It's not that." Pat shook his head. "I'm pretty sure it was Ron who got between me and Peggy back when we were young. Even when he's not around he gets in the way." He put his glass down on the table and got to his feet. "Maybe I better go." Pat extended his hand to Nick. "Thank you."

Jasmine put the Dom Perignon bottle down as Pat walked over to shake her hand as well. "I really appreciate all you did for me."

Holly got up and followed him. "Let me walk you out." As they crossed the main entry hall, she said, "Pat, it's obvious you care a great deal for Peggy, and I know she cares for you."

"Does she?" Pat asked.

"What is it with you and her?" Holly asked a touch of exasperation in her voice. "Everyone can see it but the two of you."

Pat sighed. "Maybe she cared for me once. But now? Face it. If I got cleared at the cost of her brother being found guilty, she'll never be able to look at me without thinking of that."

It was Holly's turn to sigh. "I get that, but what if Ron's not guilty?"

"I think that would be a miracle."

Holly reached for the doorknob and pulled the door open. "You may be right, but if I know my cousin, she'll be back out on that patio anytime now telling us we've got to clear her brother's name. And if we do ..."

"And if you do," Pat stepped out stepped outside and looked out across the front lawn to the stand of trees in the distance, "I still won't be good enough for Peggy Lowe."

Holly watched helplessly as he descended the stairs, got in his car and drove off.

When she returned to the patio, she found Jasmine refilling Nick and Ivy's champagne flutes. "Hey, did you save any for me?" she asked.

Jasmine held up the bottle to the light. "You're in luck. Looks like there's just enough for one more glass."

Holly located the flute she'd left on the side table and watched the sparkling liquid reach the top rim. "Cheers," she took a sip and sat down beside Nick on the couch.

Ivy frowned. "That was the least cheerful 'cheers' I've ever heard."

Holly shrugged and took another sip.

"Hey," Jasmine moved to the edge of her chair. "Did you guys get to talk to Cassie?"

"We did," Holly nodded. "That seems like days ago, not hours."

"Did she tell you anything?" Nick asked.

After recounting their visit to the Country Club, Holly said, "So I guess we just have to wait to hear from Cassie."

Violet appeared in the doorway. "Jaz, Aunt Peggy wants to talk to you."

"Duty calls." Jasmine put down her glass and followed her sister inside.

"You know, we're done here," Nick said. "We did what your cousin asked. We could go home."

Holly looked across at her sister. Ivy smiled. "Nick, Nick, Nick. You know as well as we do that any minute Peggy is going to come out here and ask us to clear her brother."

Holly grinned. "Money's no object."

48 PRIVATE DETECTIVE

Ivy jumped to her feet. "Let me go get my list of suspects."

Nick shook his head as Ivy disappeared inside. "I don't like this. Not one bit."

"I know." Holly reached for his hand and gave it a squeeze. "But aren't you happy you cleared Pat?"

"Sure, but I don't like playing private detective."

Holly screwed up her mouth. "How can you say that? You are a detective. Investigating is what you do for a living."

"Yeah, with a badge that entitles me to." Nick pinched the bridge of his nose. "Look, I'm glad we cleared Pat, but have you thought about what happens if Peggy's brother is guilty?"

"Ew!" Holly stretched out and rested her head on the back of the wicker couch. "And that is a distinct possibility."

Ivy returned to the patio with her legal pad. "I don't know why I bothered. We only had three suspects. Now that Pat's cleared, we're left with Fred and ..."

"Ron." Nick finished her sentence, shooting a penetrating look at Holly. She sat up and squirmed uncomfortably under his gaze.

Appearing relieved at the sound of the doorbell coming from inside, she said, "Maybe that's Cassie."

As she stood up, Nick grabbed her arm. "Sit down," he said, just the trace of a smile on his face. "Higgins will get it."

As she dropped back down on the couch, Higgins passed by the open French doors on his way to the entrance hall. After a few moments, he passed back in the opposite direction followed by Ronnie Lowe.

"Oh boy," Ivy said in a hushed tone. "Do you think they arrested Ron?"

"Yep," Nick leaned back and crossed his arms.

****

A few minutes later Higgins appeared on the patio. "Ms. Lowe would like to see you all in her office."

Holly quickly got up, avoiding making eye contact with Nick. The trio followed Higgins who opened the office door and stepped aside for them to enter.

Like bodyguards, Fern and Violet stood on either side of Peggy's chair. Jasmine and Ronnie sat in chairs facing them. Fighting back tears, Peggy looked at Nick. "Ronnie just informed us that Detective Jaworski has arrested my brother. Once again, I have to ask you for your help."

Nick looked from her to Ronnie. "Could you give us a minute?"

"Hold on. Anything that concerns my father concerns me." Ronnie turned to Peggy, with a questioning look.

Peggy locked eyes with Nick. After a moment she nodded. "Ronnie, please wait for us in the drawing room."

Ronnie started to speak, but then caught himself. "Yes, Aunt Peggy," he said and got up. He shot Nick an icy stare as he exited the room.

"Nick, please sit down," Peggy said, motioning to the chair Ronnie had vacated.

Nick sat down, glanced over at Jasmine, then back to Peggy. "Peg, I'm not a private detective. I'm a policeman. There's a difference. My job is not to clear someone. My job is to find the guilty party."

Jasmine made brief eye contact with Holly and Ivy who were standing near the door. All three of them knew where this conversation was headed.

Peggy sniffed. "Are you saying you think my brother is guilty?"

"No." Nick shook his head. "What we didn't discuss when I agreed to help check out the evidence against Pat Keefe is that if I found evidence against him I'd have been obligated to share it with Detective Jaworski."

"But you didn't," Peggy's voice cracked.

"Only because we didn't find any evidence against him that the police didn't already have." Nick took a deep breath. "You can't be sure of the same result this time."

Peggy balled her hands into fists. "I can't believe my brother is a murderer."

Nick reached across the desk and took Peggy's hands in his. "I understand that, but before I agree to continue investigating, I need you to know that if I turn up evidence that your brother is guilty, I *will* turn that evidence over to Jaworski."

Peggy lowered her head and let out a brief sob. When she looked back up at Nick, she said, "Find the truth. Find Hiram's killer."

49 RONNIE

"Okay, then." Nick stood up and made eye contact with Jasmine. "Let's go."

Jasmine glanced across the desk at Peggy. "Do you want to come with us?"

Peggy hesitated, her eyes reflecting her internal struggle. "No. But maybe Ronnie would."

Jasmine nodded, got to her feet and followed Nick out the door. Holly turned to Ivy and whispered, "You stay here. I want to talk to Nick before they leave."

She reached the drawing room just in time to hear Jasmine tell Ronnie that she and Nick were going to the Luzerne County Jail and ask if he wanted to go with them.

"Hold on," Ronnie said. "Why are *you* going there?"

Nick locked eyes with Ronnie but said nothing.

"Because Aunt Peggy has asked us to," Jasmine replied. "Do you want to go with us?"

"Are you going to arrange my father's bail?" Ronnie asked. "That's why I came here."

"Sorry, Ronnie. Your father has most probably been charged with first- or second-degree murder, in which case there is no bail," Jasmine explained.

"No bail!" Ronnie jumped up from the couch. "How can that be?" he shouted. "Isn't this America?"

"Yes," Nick replied, "and no bail for persons charged with first- or second-degree murder charges is the law in most of the United States, son."

"I'm not your son." Ronnie's expression changed from distraught to sardonic. "Who are you anyway?" he asked in a surly tone that reminded Holly of the boy's father.

Again, Nick said nothing as he stared coldly at the angry young man and again Jasmine answered. "This is Nick Manelli, a homicide detective with the Pineland Park, New Jersey Police Department," she said.

"New Jersey!" Ronnie scoffed. "A Country Club murder isn't exactly your milieu, is it, Detective? You do know what milieu means?"

Holly held her breath as she watched Nick. She wanted to slap Ronnie. She could only imagine how angry Nick was. But again, Nick said nothing.

Jasmine sighed loudly. "So, I take it you don't want to go with us."

"No. I don't. And I don't want you to go there either."

"Well, you don't have a choice, pal," Nick replied. "We're working for your Aunt, not you."

Ronnie raised his hand, jabbing the air with his index finger. "We'll see about that." Turning he strode out of the room, smoldering anger trailing in his wake.

Jasmine shook her head. "I can't believe that's the same guy who came over here with flowers for Aunt Peggy the other day."

"Yeah." Holly nodded. "He might have better manners in social situations than Ron, but there's no doubt — he's his father's son."

Nick let out a soft, scoffing laugh. "Hey, cut the boy some slack. He's used to getting his own way. Coming up against the legal system is always a cold, hard shock for these rich boys."

"Okay, I get that," Jasmine said, "but doesn't he realize we're trying to help his father?"

"Good question," Nick replied turning his laser gaze to Holly.

"You don't think …" Holly stopped, her brow crinkling as her eyes met his.

Jasmine watched the pair as they stared at one another, saying nothing. "What? Are you two communicating telepathically now?" she quipped.

"No," Nick said. "Holly just realized that Ronnie-boy may know something he's not telling and …"

Jasmine held up her hand, palm outward, an expression of understanding on her face. "And it may actually implicate his father."

"And," Holly continued, "he may not really want anyone competent handling the investigation."

"Okay, enough speculating," Nick said. "Let's go review the charges and evidence and talk to the man himself."

"We better move fast before Ronnie goes home to Mommy and gets us legally thrown off the case," Jasmine said, heading to the door.

"Can they do that?" Holly asked.

"Yes, they can," Nick said, following Jasmine out to the entrance hall.

"But they can't stop us from investigating on our own?" Holly said as she trailed behind.

"No," Nick gave Holly a quick kiss on the lips, "as you've

proven time and time again."

50 THE WAIT

"We'll go in my car," Nick said.

Holly watched as Jasmine followed him down the front steps to the Malibu.

"Anything we should do while you're gone?" she called after them.

"No," Nick replied as he opened the car door.

Opening the passenger side door, Jasmine said, "Text me if you hear from Cassie,"

"Right," Holly nodded.

"And just that," Nick said. "Wait here. Don't go anywhere."

Holly sighed. "Okay, okay." She waved as they drove off, then went back inside. Out on the patio Violet was showing Ivy pictures on her phone.

"And last Halloween Reed was Spiderman and Lilly was a cowgirl," Violet said.

"Oh, wow, she looks just like Holly!" When Ivy looked up and saw her sister, she waved her over. "You've got to see this picture of Violet's daughter. There's one of you in the old family albums that looks exactly the same – six-shooters and all."

Holly grinned as she glanced at the photo. "Yep, that could

be me for sure," she smiled, dropping down on a wicker chair.

"Hey, did Ronnie go with Nick and Jasmine?" Ivy asked.

"No." Holly grimaced. "And he didn't want them to go either. After he learned they weren't going to be able to bail Ron out, he pitched a fit."

"That lovely boy who brought Aunt Peggy flowers the other day?" Violet said, her expression conveying both disbelief and confusion.

"Yep." Holly's head moved up and down slowly like a bobble-head doll's. She recounted the rest of the conversation with Ronnie. "We think maybe he knows something he's not telling — something that could be harmful to Ron."

"Oh," Ivy sank back in her chair, "and he's worried Jasmine and Nick will figure it out."

"But that's just stupid," Violet frowned. "Even if Ron is guilty, Jaz needs to know the truth if she's going to mount a credible defense for him. Even I know that."

"Well, I'm not sure if she's going to get the chance. The way he ran out of here, Jasmine was worried he'd go home to his mother and get them thrown off the case. She and Nick left in a rush. They wanted to get access to the case files before that happens."

"So, what do we do?" Ivy asked.

"Wait for Cassie," Holly replied. "We have to hope she contacts Peggy and that she has information that will help us figure out why Hiram was murdered. I think finding out the why is the key to finding out who did it. By the way, where is Peggy?"

"Mom took her upstairs. She was pretty shaken after the conversation with Uncle Nick," Violet said.

Ivy sighed. "She just can't believe her brother is capable of murder. But she's clearly worried sick that he is."

Holly groaned. "I hate this. All we can do now is wait."

****

"Gin," Ivy said, laying her cards down on the table.

"You cheated!" Holly threw her cards down.

Ivy snorted. "You always say that when I win."

"You two crack me up," Violet laughed as she gathered the cards together. "Another game?"

Ivy stretched her arms over her head, moving from side to side. "What do you say we take a walk down to the greenhouse instead?"

"Oh, that sounds good," Violet said. As she placed the cards in a neat stack, Fern stepped onto the patio, her face creased with worry.

"What's the matter?" Holly asked.

"When we went upstairs before, Peggy fell asleep. I sat out on the balcony reading. I must have dozed off too. Neither of us heard the cellphone ping. When Peggy woke up a little while ago, she checked her phone. There was a text from Cassie saying she was on her way over."

"Great," Holly said.

Fern gave her head an ominous shake. "That was three hours ago."

51 RON'S DEFENSE

After reviewing the case files, Nick and Jasmine sat waiting in the same interview room where they had met with Pat Keefe. They both looked up as the door opened and an armed guard escorted a weary-looking Ron into the room. Dark circles formed half-moons under his eyes and his skin had an unhealthy pallor. He hesitated in front of the table, squinting as he eyed first Jasmine, then Nick. After a moment, he dropped into the chair facing them.

As the guard exited the room, Ron crossed his arms in front of him. "Charles told me you would be coming here. I don't know why."

"Your sister sent us," Jasmine replied, looking down at her notepad. "We're working with Charles' firm, and an attorney from his office just went over the case files with us. A gun registered to you was used to kill Hiram Thurston and to also take a shot at your sister. You had an argument with Hiram Thurston the morning he was murdered and were heard to threaten him. You also threatened your sister. You have no alibi for Thurston's time of death, nor for the evening Peggy was shot at." Looking back up at Ron, she said, "The evidence is pretty damning. You got anything for us to help mount a defense for you?"

Ron sighed. "I never threatened Hiram."

"You don't consider the words," Jasmine looked down at her legal pad and read, "'Do this and you'll regret it' a threat?" She looked back up at Ron. "Those words?"

Ron lowered his eyes to the table surface. "I never said that."

Jasmine turned and shot a frustrated glance at Nick.

Nick placed both hands flat on the table and leaned towards Ron. "Your sister sent us here because she thinks you're innocent of the charges, and she wants us to prove that. Me? I think you're guilty as hell and I couldn't care less if you rot in jail for the rest of your miserable life." Nick sat up and smiled. "But here's the thing. Whether you work with us or somebody else, I assure you that with the case the DA has against you, denying something that's been reported by credible witnesses is not a defense."

Ron just stared back at Nick.

Jasmine tapped the table with her pen. "You do understand you've been charged with first degree murder and in the state of Pennsylvania, the punishment for a first-degree conviction is either death or mandatory life in prison without the possibility of parole?"

Ron blinked as he turned his gaze to Jasmine. Her words appeared to have broken through his unresponsive veneer. He uncrossed his arms and shifted in his chair.

"So, what do you want me to tell you?" he asked, this time, his tone more resigned than combative.

"The truth," Jasmine replied. "What did you and Hiram argue about the morning he was murdered?"

Ron's eyes darted from Jasmine to Nick and back again. "Okay. He came to tell us he discovered some financial irregularities with the Country Club's bookkeeping, and he was going to call a special meeting of the Board of Directors requesting an outside audit of the books."

"What kind of irregularities?" Jasmine asked.

"That's just it. He wouldn't tell me. He claimed he came by to see if I had anything I'd like to tell him before he called the meeting. Can you believe that?" Ron pounded the table.

"What exactly did you say to him?" Jasmine flipped a page in her notebook and sat with her pen poised.

"I told him to hold on. Give me a chance to review the books myself, but he refused."

"And you objected?" Jasmine asked.

"Of course, I objected. I'm the Board Treasurer. Anything wrong would reflect on me. I'm supposed to review the financials and our bank accounts on an on-going basis."

"Supposed to?" Nick frowned. "Did you?"

Ron squinted as he looked past Nick, appearing lost in thought.

"Well," Jasmine prompted. "Did you? It's a simple yes or no question."

Ron cleared his throat. "Yes — of course, I did. That's why I didn't understand what Hiram was talking about."

"Why wouldn't he allow you to review the books before calling for an audit?" Jasmine asked.

"Oh, he said something about transparency and ethics and wanting our handling of this to be beyond reproach," Ron smirked. "That kind of crap."

Jasmine scratched the back of her head. "Where were you the afternoon Hiram was murdered?

"Like I told Jaworski, I drove out to the lake and took a ride on my boat. It's what I do when I just want to get away from everybody."

"Anyone see you?"

"Who knows? I didn't talk to anybody. I wasn't thinking I

needed an alibi."

"And the night Peggy was shot at? The report says you were home asleep, but your wife couldn't confirm that." Jasmine pursed her lips.

Ron appeared annoyed. "Look, plenty of people have separate bedrooms."

"Were you at the coronation of the Supreme Commander?" Jasmine waggled her head, her voice laced with sarcasm.

Ron jerked his head back. "How do you know about that?"

"Were you there?" Jasmine asked.

"Yes."

Jasmine turned to Nick. "Any questions, Detective?"

Nick nodded. "How'd your gun get in Pat Keefe's truck?"

Ron again pounded the table with both fists. "That's another thing. I have no idea how it got there. I keep that gun in the glovebox of my car. I never used it, except at the practice range and I haven't been there in months. I don't even remember the last time I opened the glovebox."

"Was the glovebox locked?" Nick asked.

"Maybe." Ron shrugged. "I rarely lock the car. I honestly don't know."

"Anyone else know where you kept the gun?" Jasmine asked.

"Uh ..." Ron stared at Jasmine a few seconds before he answered. "No. No one."

Jasmine gave a sidelong look at Nick as she jotted something on her pad.

"One last question." Nick again leaned forward. "Did you kill Hiram Thurston?"

Unblinking, Ron met Nick's steely gaze. "No," was all he said.

52 PETE SMITH

A worried look on her face, Peggy hurried out onto the patio. "I finally got through to someone in the kitchen at the Country Club. All they could tell me was that Cassie wasn't there. We have to do something."

"Do you want us to take a drive over there?" Holly asked.

"Yes," Ivy nodded. "We can drive the same route she would have taken to get here."

"Oh, I pray she didn't have an accident," Peggy said, her eyes filling up.

Ivy patted Peggy's arm. "Don't think that. Maybe she just had a flat tire."

Peggy nodded. "You're right. I'll come with you."

Fern put a restraining hand on Peggy's arm. "No. We'll stay here. We need to be here in case Cassie does show up."

"Mom's right," Violet added. "It's possible she had to stop somewhere and just got delayed. I'll stay with you."

"Okay," Peggy relented, turning to Holly. "But please. Hurry. And call us the minute you know something."

****

"This is not good," Holly said as she pulled out on to the

main road.

"I know, but let's not get ahead of ourselves," Ivy said, looking out at the road ahead. "Maybe she really did have a flat tire."

"And didn't text to let us know?"

"Her phone could be out of charge," Ivy suggested.

Holly's ponytail bounced as she shook her head. "Yeah, and her Fairy Godmother could have whisked her away to the ball."

"Please try to stay positive," Ivy pleaded.

"I can't help it," Holly said. "Since Peggy mentioned an accident, I can't stop thinking about what happened to Teresa Nowicki."

"Oh gosh!" Ivy blew air through her lips. "This is different, Holly."

"Really? Cassie was on her way to tell us something that might help discover a murderer. That's exactly what Teresa was doing when she got run off the road and almost killed."

"Slow down please," Ivy said. "We're almost there and our getting in an accident would not help anyone."

Holly lifted her foot from the accelerator. "That's exactly what I said to Peggy when we left this place this morning." Holly sighed. "Oh no!"

"What?"

"I just remembered Nick said to wait for Cassie at the house and not to go anywhere."

"Oh please," Ivy scoffed. "And when have you ever let that stop you?"

Holly laughed in spite of herself. In just a few minutes, they arrived at the Country Club.

"There's a parking spot right near the front entrance," Ivy

said.

"But we're not going in the front entrance," Holly replied turning onto the road marked "Deliveries only". "I think we have a better chance of learning something from the back-of-house workers."

"You're right," Ivy agreed. "The last person I want to run into is Fred Locksley."

They followed the winding service road, arriving at a single-bay loading dock.

"We're in luck," Holly said when she spotted three men sitting on plastic chairs outside of what was most likely the kitchen door. Two of the men appeared Hispanic. The third was a middle-aged white man, smoking a cigarette. All three wore white aprons. The youngest looking of the trio got up and headed to the door as Holly brought the car to a stop. The remaining two sat, just watching as Holly and Ivy got out of the car and walked over.

"You take a wrong turn, *señoras*," the Hispanic man said smiling at them.

Holly smiled back. "No. We actually wanted to talk to you."

"Well, aren't we lucky, Pedro," the older man said. "Two pretty ladies want to talk to us. Are you twins?"

"No," Ivy replied. "We get that all the time."

"Whadaya know? You even sound alike," the man smiled. "What can we do for you?"

"We're looking for Cassie Snyder. Have either of you guys seen her?"

The smile left the Hispanic man's face. "No, *señora. Mi ingles* no so good." He stood up, glancing nervously at the windows above the back door. "*Con permiso*," he said and hurried to the door.

Holly turned to the older man, who took a final draw on

THE BLOOMING TREASURE MURDER

his cigarette and dropped it in what was left in a coffee cup he was holding.

Slowly he got up, and speaking loudly said, "Let me show you to your car, ladies." With his back turned to the building, he winked at Holly, took her by the elbow and guided her back towards the car. Ivy followed.

In a whisper he said, "I'm Pete Smith, a friend of Pat Keefe's." Pointing in the opposite direction from where they had just come, he continued. "Around one o'clock, I saw Cassie talking to Fred Locksley out by her car. They looked like they were arguing."

As they reached the car, Holly turned to face Pete, nodding, giving him a big smile in return. Faking a laugh, she covered her mouth with her hand. "Did she leave alone?"

"I don't know," the man nodded, continuing to point as if he were giving her directions. "One of Locksley's cronies came into the kitchen, and I had to move away from the window. But I haven't seen either of them since."

Ivy feigned a giggle, turned her back to the building and asked, "What type of car does she drive?"

"A black Kia," Pete replied, then turned to face her, shaking his head, grinning.

Holly faked another laugh as she got back in the car. "Thank you," she said, closing the door, waving as she drove back up the road in the direction Pete had pointed.

When they arrived at the front of the Country Club, "Ivy lifted her chin towards a row of reserved parking spaces. "There's Locksley's car."

Holly scanned the lot. "No sign of a black Kia," she said, heading toward the exit. "Get out my phone and ..."

"I know. I know. Call Nick."

53 BAD NEWS

"Well, we don't have good news," Holly said as she and Ivy entered the entrance hall of the Lowe Estate.

Frowning, Violet held the door open for them. "We don't either."

"No word from Cassie?" Ivy asked.

"I'll let Aunt Peggy read you the text she sent after you left," Violet replied and headed to the drawing room where Peggy and Fern sat waiting.

"Any luck?" Peggy asked, looking momentarily hopeful.

"No, but read us this text Violet told us about."

Peggy picked up her phone, tapped the screen and read, "I won't be able to make it after all, Ms. Lowe. Just wanted you to know that I rechecked something after you and your cousin left. I was mistaken. Cassie."

"I don't know about you," Fern sneered, "but I'm not buying it."

Holly and Ivy exchanged a worried look. "Neither do we," said Holly, dropping down in an armchair.

"Yeah," Ivy agreed. "Especially since Cassie was seen out in the parking lot arguing with Locksley around one o'clock."

"Oh no!" Peggy jumped to her feet. "That must have been right after she texted me. If anything happens to her, it's all my fault," she said, balling her hands into fists.

Fern grabbed her wrist and tugged. "Sit down. Something very wrong is going on at that snake pit you call a Country Club and none of it is your fault."

Peggy sank back down. "We have to do something." She aimed a pleading look at Holly.

"Nick and Jasmine texted they're on their way back," Holly said. "Let's wait for them."

"Did they say how it went with Ron?" Violet asked.

"No." Holly replied.

"So, we just wait?" Peggy asked, her tone one part frustrated, one part resigned.

"Well, there is one thing." Ivy sat down beside Holly. "I'm assuming you tried calling Cassie after you got the text."

"Yes," Peggy said, "but it went straight to voice mail."

"If Cassie's not at the Country Club, she probably went home," Ivy continued. "We could drive there. Does she live nearby?"

"Oh, why didn't I think of that?" Peggy again reached for her phone. "She lives with her mother. I think I have her number in my contact list. Yes, yes. Here it is." She tapped the phone and waited. "Hi, Eileen. This is Peggy Lowe. Is Cassie there?"

Peggy's hopeful expression quickly turned to one of disappointment. "I see. Uh-huh. Thanks anyway." Peggy appeared on the verge of tears. "She said Cassie left to visit a friend in Vermont. She's not sure when she'll be back."

"At least, we know she's safe," Violet said soothingly.

"Yes, but Locksley got to her." Fern pursed her lips.

"Got to whom?" Jasmine asked as she entered the drawing

room, Nick behind her.

"Oh, thank heaven you two are back," Holly said, sliding over to make room for Nick on the couch.

"We've got nothing but bad news for you, I'm afraid," Peggy said as Jasmine sat down beside her. "I hope you have something better to tell us."

"Not really," Jasmine frowned. "Why don't you go first?"

"Well …" Holly began.

Fern put out her arm signaling Holly to stop. "Let me. You'll take too long." Fern launched into a no-nonsense account of the facts. She covered what happened from Cassie's first text up to the call to her mother, including Holly and Ivy's visit to the Country Club in under two minutes.

"Nice summation." Jasmine gave her mother an approving smile and proceeded to recount their interview with Ron. When she finished, everyone got quiet.

After a few minutes, Peggy said, "Nick, you haven't said anything. What are you thinking?"

"Me?" Nick inhaled deeply and released the air through his lips. "Well, I just have two questions. One, isn't it time for lunch? And …" He put his arm around Holly, gently grasping the back of her neck. "Two, didn't I tell you to wait here for Cassie and not go anywhere?"

54 BABY, IT'S YOU

"That's my fault, Nick," Peggy said, looking like a puppy who'd missed the wee-wee pad. "They only went because I was so worried about Cassie."

As Nick let out a weary sigh, Peggy jumped to her feet. "Fern, Violet, come with me. Let's go see if we can help Mrs. Higgins get lunch ready."

When they left the room, Jasmine looked at Nick. "You going to tell them what you really think?" she asked lifting her chin in the direction of Holly and Ivy.

"Well," Ivy moved to the edge of her seat, "are you?"

After a moment, Nick nodded. "Look, it's clear that Hiram Thurston discovered someone was embezzling funds from the Country Club. Ron claims he asked Hiram to let him review the books before he took whatever he found to the Board. That could indicate he really didn't know what was going on, in spite of the fact that he was supposed to be reviewing the Club's finances. He hedged when I asked him if he did. Even if he isn't part of the embezzlement scheme, I think he knows, or at least suspects, who is."

"But if that's true, why wouldn't he tell you?" Ivy asked.

"Could be he's protecting someone," Nick replied.

"Or, like Cassie, he's afraid of someone," Holly added.

"Either way, it's got to be Locksley, no?" Ivy asked.

Jasmine nodded. "He is the most likely suspect."

"But we've talked about this before," Holly said. "He is so not a scary guy. Really, who'd be intimidated by him?"

"But he is," Nick hesitated, "what did you call him? Supreme Leader?"

"Supreme Commander," Jasmine corrected with a grin.

"And he's got the Brothers of the Blaze behind him," Ivy added.

Jasmine pursed her lips, appearing skeptical. "But they didn't impress me as particularly dangerous either."

"I suppose if there's enough money at stake, anyone can be dangerous." Ivy frowned.

"You also don't know what Locksley might have on any of them," Nick said.

Holly sat forward. "You mean he could be blackmailing Ron, forcing him to divert funds to the brotherhood?"

"Bingo," Nick said.

"You managed to get Ron to open up a bit to you," Ivy said. "Any chance you could convince him it's in his best interest to tell you the whole truth?"

As Nick shrugged, Jasmine's phone chirped. "Jasmine Brennan here," she answered. "I see." Her brow creased as she listened. "Okay. We'll talk to Aunt Peggy."

"More bad news?" Holly asked as Jasmine tapped her screen to end the call.

"That was Charles. He said Beverly called to inform him that she is retaining another criminal law firm to represent Ron. She also informed the prosecutor that we are no longer allowed to meet with Ron."

"We knew that was coming," Nick said.

Ivy groaned. "Well, that answers my question. If you can't even talk to Ron, how are we ever going to find out what hold Locksley has over him?"

"You heard me say I'd talk to Aunt Peggy," Jasmine said. "They can't stop her from seeing him."

"And he wouldn't refuse to see his sister," Ivy said. "Would he?"

"I think the question is will she see him," Nick replied. "Remember, she didn't want to go with us this morning?"

"Right," Holly nodded. "And she's probably not going to be very helpful getting him to confess some peccadillo that Locksley's using to coerce him into cooking the books."

Jasmine locked eyes with Holly. "But what if we can convince her it's the only way to help him?"

Now Ivy turned to Holly. "Do we have any other choice?"

Holly turned to Nick and moaned when she saw he was looking at her with the same degree of expectation. "Why are you all looking at me?"

Nick kissed her on the cheek. "Well, I am because I love you, but I think your niece and sister here think if anyone can convince Peggy to talk to Ron — like the song says — Baby, it's you."

55 THE NINTH CIRCLE

As they sat in the lobby of the Luzerne County Jail, Peggy fidgeted in her chair and turned to face Holly. "Are you sure this is the right thing to do?" she asked.

Holly grimaced. "Nick and Jasmine are sure it is."

As her cousin rolled her hands compulsively, Holly realized that until that moment she had never really seen anyone "wring their hands".

"Surely, there's got to be another way to get at the truth," Peggy said, an air of desperation in her voice.

"The only other way would be if someone at the Country Club would talk to us. After what happened with Cassie, that's not very likely. Just try to relax."

"Right." Peggy's head bobbed nervously as she grasped Holly's hand. "You will come in with me?"

"Yes, of course I will."

Peggy took a deep breath, closed her eyes and became still as if she were in a meditative trance. Feeling a bit relieved, Holly also closed her eyes for a moment, wondering what, if anything, Ron would tell his sister. Could it be possible he really was innocent?

The sound of a metal door opening caused both Holly and

Peggy to open their eyes, just in time to see Beverly and Ronnie walk through the door. Beverly's expression hardened when she spotted them. She leaned in close to her son and said something to which he responded with a nod.

Peggy got to her feet and headed in their direction. Not sure that was a good idea, Holly rose and followed her anyway.

"Ron doesn't want to see you," Beverly said as Peggy drew near. Without stopping, she rushed past her sister-in-law in the direction of the exit.

Peggy ran alongside her. "But I want to see him."

Beverly stopped and glared at her. About to walk away again, she instead turned back and got just inches from Peggy's face. "You want to see him? You want to see a broken man? How dare you when this is all your fault," she snarled.

"My fault?" Peggy looked as if she'd been slapped. "How could it be my fault?"

"The police had their man — Pat Keefe. You had to go and bring your niece and that Italian detective in and now my husband is …" Beverly's chin trembled.

"But Pat is innocent," Peggy protested.

"Is he?" Beverly sneered. "Or did you just use some of that inheritance money to pay someone off to clear your — your prospect as you called him?"

"Beverly! How could you say that? I would never do such a thing. And I would never do anything that would harm Ron. You know that."

"Until recently, I would have thought I did know that." Beverly shifted her focus to Holly, shooting her a withering glance. "I thought we were family, but now that you've got your cousins, it's clear where your loyalties lie." She turned to her son. "Get rid of them." She practically spit out the words, then headed out the door.

As the exit door closed, Ronnie faced his aunt, an apologetic look on his face. "It's over. I'm sorry to tell you this, Aunt Peggy, but Dad just confessed."

"What?" Peggy staggered as both Ronnie and Holly caught hold of her.

"Let's get her to a chair," Holly said.

After they got Peggy seated, Holly asked, "What did your father confess to? Murdering Hiram?"

"Yes." Ronnie replied barely above a whisper. "I know — I can't believe it myself."

"What reason did he give?" Holly asked as Peggy started to weep.

Ronnie glanced down at the floor. "He just wants to spare me and my mother." His voice cracked as he shook his head. "I'm sorry, but I just can't ..." Turning abruptly, he strode across the lobby and disappeared out the door.

Holly sank down in the chair beside her cousin.

"Is she right?" Peggy sobbed. "Is this my fault?"

"Of course it's not your fault," Holly soothed, putting an arm around her.

Peggy dried her eyes. "I have to see him."

Before Holly could say anything, a woman in uniform came from behind the plexiglass-protected reception desk.

"Ms. Lowe?" she asked looking from Holly to Peggy.

Peggy sat up and dabbed at her eyes with a tissue. "That's me."

"Ron Lowe just informed us that he will not speak to any additional visitors today."

"But ..."

"I'm sorry." The uniformed woman gave Peggy's shoulder

a light pat, then pivoted and returned to the reception desk.

As Peggy again began to sob, Holly shivered. This was not fresh hell. No, she felt as if they had just descended into the Ninth Circle of Dante's Inferno, a frozen place lacking any warmth at all, reserved for those who have betrayed the trust of someone close and special.

56 A SURPRISE PHONE CALL

"You're not going to believe this," Jasmine said stepping out onto the patio, her cellphone in her hand.

"Was that Holly? Did they get to talk to Ron?" Ivy asked.

"No, they didn't, but," Jasmine shook her head, turning to Nick, "Ron confessed to the murder of Hiram Thurston."

Fern smirked. "Doesn't surprise me that he's guilty, but I admit I am surprised he confessed."

"Why would he do that?" Ivy asked.

"Aunt Holly said Ronnie told them he wanted to 'spare me and my mother'." Jasmine made air quotes around the words.

"So, it's over?" Violet asked.

Jasmine shrugged and again glanced at her uncle. "You're not saying anything, Uncle Nick. Why?"

Nick gave his head a slight shake. "He didn't do it."

"What?" Fern's face reflected total disbelief.

"Why do you say that?" Ivy asked.

"There are two reasons he'd confess to spare his family," Nick replied. "Like we said before, either he's being blackmailed and whatever it's about would be a real scandal for them. Or, one of them murdered Hiram."

"What possible motive do Beverly or Ronnie have for murdering Hiram Thurston?" Violet asked.

"Just because we don't know it, doesn't mean there isn't one," Jasmine replied.

"Oh, I believe Beverly might murder someone just to watch them die," Fern said.

"Thank you, Johnny Cash," Jasmine teased.

Violet looked at her mother the same way she would at one of her misbehaving children. "Now, Mom, we know you don't like her, but don't you think you're rushing to judgement?"

Suddenly Jasmine's phone chirped. Everyone got quiet as she tapped the screen. "Jasmine Brennan." Her face registered surprise. "Hi, Pat. Yeah. Uh-huh. It's a little late." She grimaced glancing at her watch. "Okay. We can be there in about fifteen minutes."

"Well?" Fern asked.

Jasmine looked at Nick. "Pat says he needs to talk to us, and it can't wait until tomorrow. All he'd say was that it's extremely important and he didn't want to talk about it on the phone."

Nick got to his feet. "We'll take ..."

"Your car. I know," Jasmine grabbed her bag.

****

"Thanks for coming so fast," Pat said as he held the door open for Jasmine and Nick. He scanned the street before closing the door. After turning the deadbolt lock, he led them into a small, but comfortable sitting room where a man sat waiting.

"This is my friend, Pete Smith. He's the cook at the Country Club I told you about," Pat said. "Pete, meet Jasmine Brennan and Nick Manelli."

As they shook hands, Nick said, "You're the guy who told

my wife you saw Cassie Snyder arguing with Fred Locksley today."

"That was your wife?"

"And my sister-in-law with her," Nick added.

Pete smiled, "Gutsy ladies."

Nick nodded. "Unfortunately."

"Have a seat," Pat said. "Pete came to me because he over-heard Locksley on the phone. I didn't know what to do. I hope you don't mind I called you."

Nick just nodded, then turned to Pete. "What did you hear?"

"Two things, actually," Pete said. "I went outside for a smoke. The window to Locksley's office is right above the spot where we take our breaks. I heard Locksley say all sinister-like, 'Now you wouldn't want anyone to find out what you did, would you? You see what happened to Ron Lowe'." Pete ran his hand through his hair. "It gave me the creeps, I tell ya."

"What else did he say?" Jasmine asked.

"Are you kidding? After the thing with Cassie, I didn't stick around to hear any more. I mean if Locksley knew I heard him..." Pete shook his head. "Look, since Mr. Thurston got mur-dered, we're all scared we're either gonna get canned — or worse," he said, his face reflecting genuine fear.

"You said you heard two things," Nick prompted.

"Oh, yeah. It gets worse. This time I was carryin' a tray of silverware and napkins to the main dining hall. We're settin' up for a wedding tomorrow. Anyways, I put the tray on a table, then notice my shoelace is untied. I bend down to tie it, and when I do, Locksley comes into the room, and he's on his cellphone." Pete moved to the edge of his chair. "This time he doesn't sound sinister. No, sir. This time he sounds like the scared little piece of shit he is."

Pete caught himself and looked apologetically at Jasmine. "Excuse my language."

"I've heard worse," Jasmine assured him.

Nodding, Pete continued. "So, he says, 'I know. I know. Don't worry. We'll get it back. I promise. Yes, whatever it takes'." He looked from Jasmine to Nick. "He started walking in my direction and I nearly peed myself, I tell ya. I figured I was a dead man If he knew I heard him. I was afraid to breathe. Lucky for me, somebody called him from the hallway. He turned and went back the way he came. But here's the thing what really raised the hair on the back of my neck. The last thing he said was 'the girl will turn over the ledger as soon as she finds out what we've got'."

57 HELP

Holly sat alone in the drawing room sipping a beer, trying to relax after the tearful drive back from the Luzerne County Jail. Poor Peggy! What a horrible turn of events. All she wanted was to bring the Donnelly family back together. She succeeded at that, but now the Lowe side of her family was torn apart. Whether Ron was guilty or not, Holly couldn't see a good final outcome. She looked up as Ivy walked into the room.

"How is she?"

"She's resting," Ivy replied. "I found a mild sedative in the medicine cabinet. Fern said she'll stay with her." Sitting down on the couch opposite her sister, she asked, "How are you?"

"Oh, I'm fine." Holly frowned as she looked to the window. "It's getting dark. I'll be a lot better when Nick and Jasmine get back. Tell me again what Pat wanted."

Ivy recounted the brief conversation Jasmine had with Pat.

Holly shook her head. "I don't like it."

"Well, it had to be important, otherwise why would he insist they come over tonight?" Ivy asked.

The doorbell rang and the two sisters both jumped to their feet.

"Thank God we don't have to wait any longer to get the answer to that question," Holly said as they headed to the entrance hall, where they met with Higgins who was on his way to open the door. "It's okay, Higgins. We've got this." The butler stopped, but waited as she reached for the door, pulling it wide open. When she did, she was surprised to see, not Nick and Jasmine, but Cassie Snyder. "Oh," was all she said.

Cassie's hair was disheveled, and her eyes were puffy and red. A black, vinyl backpack hung from her shoulder. She looked years older than the young woman Holly and Peggy had visited at the Country Club that morning. "Please. Can I come in?" she asked, casting a nervous glance over her shoulder.

"Of course." Ivy quickly moved forward, took the distraught girl by the arm and pulled her inside.

Holly scanned the drive before she pulled the door shut and bolted it.

"Anything I can do?" Higgins asked, appearing as disconcerted as Holly felt.

"I'll let you know." Holly gave him a grateful smile.

"We'll set another place for dinner, just in case," he replied and headed back to the kitchen.

Holly entered the drawing room in time to see Cassie sink onto the couch. Her arms tightly wrapped around her backpack, she lowered her head and sobbed. Ivy dropped down and put a comforting arm around the girl. Holly grabbed the nearly empty tissue box and placed it on the coffee table in front of them.

The sisters exchanged a knowing glance. They'd comforted enough troubled friends and family members to know they needed to let Cassie cry until she was ready to talk.

After a few sobs and sniffles, Cassie looked up. "Is Ms. Lowe here?"

"I just gave her a sedative," Ivy said, explaining about Ron's confession.

"Oh, this is turning into a nightmare," Cassie said, dabbing at the tears she seemed unable to stop. After a moment, she stood up. "I'm sorry. I shouldn't have come here. You folks have enough of your own problems."

Holly got up. "Cassie, wait. Please," she said her voice soft and soothing. The girl stopped and faced her. "You remember me. I came to your office this morning with Peggy."

"Yes, of course." Cassie nodded. "You're her cousin."

"That's right. We came to you for help, and now you need our help. That means you realize all of these problems are linked."

Cassie again nodded as Holly motioned to the couch. "Come sit back down."

As Cassie returned to the couch, Holly continued. "This is my sister, Ivy. You know Peggy trusts us. So can you. Now, why don't you tell us why you came here."

"Yes," Ivy nodded. "We'll do whatever we can to help you."

"That's just it. I don't know if anyone can help me at this point." Cassie closed her eyes and let out a small groan. When she reopened her eyes, she said, "I don't know. I'd feel better if I could talk to Ms. Lowe."

"Well, that's not going to happen." Fern stood in the doorway. "We just managed to get her to sleep."

Fern walked into the room, eyed Cassie, then turned to her sisters. "I heard the doorbell. Who's this?"

"Cassie Snyder," Ivy replied. Turning to the young woman, she said, "This is our sister, Fern."

"Well, young lady," Fern said sternly. "You look quite a mess, so I'm guessing something derailed your trip to Vermont. Why did you come to see Peggy and not go home to your own mother?"

Cassie sniffed. "Because they've kidnapped my mother."

58 THE LEDGER

Fern sank down on the sofa next to Holly as Cassie again covered her face with her hands.

"You've been contacted by the kidnappers?" Holly asked.

Cassie nodded. Cradling the backpack in one arm, she reached for a tissue with the other. After blowing her nose, she said, "I was driving about an hour when my phone rang. I didn't think much of it and figured I'd check the message whenever I felt like a rest stop. After about another fifteen minutes, the phone rang again. It was only another few miles to a rest stop, so I pulled in and checked my phone. The voice message said if I wanted to see my mother alive again, I'd return what I took."

"And what was that?" Holly asked.

Cassie hesitated. After a moment she centered the backpack in her lap. She released the snaps and unzipped the top panel. Slowly, she pulled out a book. The cover was speckled with multi-colored spots, and it had a red ribbon visible at the top, a kind of book marker you used to see in old-fashioned prayer books and Bibles.

"I once had a diary that looked exactly like that," Fern said as they sat staring at the book.

"Is that what it is?" Ivy asked. "A diary."

Cassie shook her head. "No. It's a ledger."

"May I see it?" Holly asked.

Cassie handed it to her and Holly opened to the first page, Fern looking over her shoulder.

"Oh, brother," Holly said under her breath.

"What is it?" Ivy asked.

Holly fanned the pages and looked across at her sister. "A running list of initials and dollar amounts."

Fern took the book from Holly and flipped through the pages. "It's color-coded, too. Some entries are in blue. Others are green." Fern looked up. "The larger numbers are green."

"If you open to where the red ribbon marker is, you'll see a different kind of list," Cassie said. "Two columns of numbers. The figures correspond to the amounts in some questionable invoices I discovered."

"In each case the second column is a few thousand lower than the first column," Fern said.

"The difference between a real invoice and a payoff?" Ivy asked.

"I think so," Cassie said. "A few weeks ago, I got suspicious after I received an invoice that was higher than an estimate we'd received for some landscaping materials. I just happened to remember the estimated amount because Mr. Thurston and I discussed what a good deal we'd gotten. But then I started checking files and saw that there were several contractors or suppliers whose invoices were higher than their original estimates, all approved by Mr. Locksley. That's why I went to Mr. Thurston with the information."

"Did you have this ledger this morning when we visited you?" Holly asked.

"No," Cassie replied. "After you left, the mail arrived and there was a padded envelope addressed to me. Inside was this."

SALLY HANDLEY

She detached the Velcro fastener holding down the front pocket of the backpack and extracted an old-fashioned silver key.

"You knew what the key was for?" Ivy asked.

"There was a note," Cassie's chin trembled. "It was from Hiram. It said, 'This opens the bottom drawer of the wooden cabinet in the storage room. If anything happens to me, give it to the police.'"

"Oh girl, what have you done?" Fern shook her head slightly from side to side.

"I know — I know," Cassie's face was a portrait of regret. "After you and Peggy left, Mr. Locksley grilled me about our conversation. He finally let me go, but I felt like he was still suspicious. Anyway, he said he had to go out for an hour. The mail arrived just as he was leaving. When I saw the key, I remembered seeing Mr. Locksley going in and out of the storage room with a key like that." She gave her shoulders a repentant shrug. "I just wanted to know what was in the drawer, so I went into the storage room. I found the ledger and leafed through it. That's when I discovered the two columns of figures and realized they corresponded to the estimates and invoices I'd questioned."

"And you thought it was a good idea to steal a ledger that could be evidence in a murder investigation instead of turning the key over to the police like Hiram instructed you to?" Fern scowled at the girl.

"Look, I intended to bring the ledger here for Ms. Lowe to give to the police," Cassie said. "I locked the cabinet back up and stuffed the ledger in my backpack. Unfortunately, Mr. Locksley returned just as I was getting into my car to come over here. He started questioning me again about your visit this morning. He threatened me. He said if I dared talk about Country Club business, I'd regret it. He actually said, 'you saw what happened to Hiram'." Cassie flailed her hands, her expression desperate. "I didn't even go home. I called my mother and said I was going to my friend's place in Vermont, and I'd call her when I arrived."

"Why didn't you come straight here?" Holly asked.

"I don't know. I wasn't thinking straight," Cassie replied, tears again starting down her cheeks in jagged streams.

"Clearly," Fern huffed.

"You're not helping here, Fern." Holly shot her sister an admonishing look.

Ivy patted Cassie on the knee. "Let's get back to the call from the kidnapper. Did you actually speak with him?"

Cassie nodded. "I called back the number and the man who answered said to go home — that they'd call me again with instructions about where to return what I took."

"Did you get to talk to your mother?" Holly asked.

Cassie stifled a sob. "Yes. She just said 'I'm all right.'"

Holly scratched the back of her head. "Okay. Jasmine and Nick should be back soon. Let's wait for …"

She stopped as Cassie's cellphone chirped.

59 BIRNAM WOOD

"Put the call on speaker," Holly said.

Cassie tapped the screen. "Hello."

"Are you back home?" a muffled voice asked.

Cassie looked to Holly who nodded.

"Yes, I'm home."

"Okay. You have twenty minutes to get to the Country Club. Park in front. A golf cart will be waiting for you there. Drive it out to the Temple behind the ninth hole of the golf course."

"Wait. Twenty minutes. I can't ..."

"Twenty minutes, and I don't need to tell you to come alone." The caller disconnected.

Cassie made a frantic reach for the ledger. As she stuffed it in her backpack, Holly said, "We'll come with you."

"No!" Cassie's eyes had a wild look. "You heard him." She got up and ran out the door before anyone could stop her.

"You know they're going to kill her and her mother too, once they get that ledger," Fern said.

Holly nodded. "But if we go the back way, we can probably get there before her,"

"What are we waiting for?" Ivy headed to the door not waiting for an answer.

Higgins intercepted them in the entrance hall. "Going out ladies?"

"Yes. When Jasmine and Nick get here tell them they need to meet us at the bonfire site," Holly said as the three sisters hurried out the door.

****

As she sped along the main road, Holly said, "Okay. In the trunk I have an umbrella and a window scraper."

"Concerned about a weather event, are you?" Fern asked in her surliest tone.

"Fern!" Holly said unable to contain her exasperation. "They're the closest thing I have to weapons in this car. Tell her Ivy."

"Oh yeah. Our friend, Kate. She'll face wild animals with nothing more than a broom. Wait a second," Ivy said, excitement in her voice. "Is this a fanny pack back here?"

"Perfect," Holly said. "I was looking for that. I forgot I stuffed it back there. This is great!"

"A backpack is great? What am I missing?" Fern asked, her voice a tad less brusque.

"Demonstrate for her, Ivy," Holly said.

"Okay. Now listen very carefully and tell me what this sounds like." Ivy connected the two plastic ends of the fanny pack straps together.

Fern cast a sidelong look at Holly. "I don't even want to know how you two figured out that click sounds exactly like a trigger being cocked."

"Long story," Holly said shaking her head. "Look, when we get there, you'll stay with the car like last time."

"You really think that's a good idea?" Fern asked.

"Yeah," Ivy leaned forward resting her arms on the backs of the front seats. "Maybe we should all stay together."

"No," Holly said, her voice commanding. "Someone's got to be able to — to tell Nick and Jasmine where to go when they get here."

"Jasmine knows the way," Fern replied.

Holly shook her head. "Fern, you know why you need to stay here. Don't make me say it."

"In case something goes wrong, I need to tell the tale," Fern said softly.

"Yeah," Holly said barely above a whisper.

A few seconds later Ivy asked, "Are we almost there?"

"Yes," Fern replied. "Slow down." After a few more yards, she said, "Stop."

Holly pulled over, turned off the ignition and popped the trunk. She and Ivy got out and went around to the back of the car. Handing the umbrella to Ivy, Holly said, "Give me the fanny pack." She tossed it over her shoulder and grabbed the long-armed window scraper.

"Be careful," Fern said through the open passenger window.

Holly nodded. "Close that window and lock the doors." She looped her arm through Ivy's. They heard the sound of the window sliding shut and the door locks clicking in place as they started up the service road.

After they walked for a few minutes, Ivy whispered, "I'd be lying if I didn't' say I was scared."

"Me too," Holly whispered back.

"We don't even have a plan."

"I know and we're really just going to have to wing it. A

lot depends on how many people we're going to be facing. One or two and we've got a chance against them. If there's more, all we can do is try to put a monkey wrench in their plans and slow them down until Nick gets here."

After another few minutes, Ivy asked. "How much further is it?"

"The clearing is just up ahead. Something's different than last time, though," Holly said. As they drew nearer to the opening onto the golf course, she saw that a huge pile of branches was stacked across the service road. They would have to make their way through the wooded area to get on the golf course the same way she and Jasmine had the night of the bonfire.

When they reached the pile of branches, Holly pointed. "There's the Temple. It's hard to see from here. Last time the bonfire lit up the place."

"You think they've got Cassie's mother inside?" Ivy asked.

"Maybe."

"If we're going to be of any help, we need to get closer," Ivy said. "But how can we get closer without exposing ourselves?"

"Good question." Holly frowned. After a moment she gave her fingers a noiseless snap. "I've got it." She grabbed hold of a branch on the pile and started to tug. "Help me," she said.

Ivy grasped a branch on the opposite side of the shrub Holly had hold of. Together they yanked loose the remains of a dead shrub about four feet in diameter at its widest part.

"Yep, this will do," Holly said. "We need another one the same size."

"I don't get it," Ivy said.

"Ah, that's because you never read Macbeth." Holly reached for the bottom branch of another shrub in the pile.

"I did see the play in college," Ivy said, again grasping a branch on the opposite side.

"Do you remember the prediction about Birnam Wood?"

"Oh, yeah!" Ivy said as she tugged. "I remember now. That's the part where the soldiers camouflage themselves as trees to get closer to Macbeth's castle."

As they pulled the second shrub loose, Ivy turned to Holly. "Do you really think this will work?"

Holly squeezed her sister's hand. "It's got to."

60 EAVESDROPPING

"Well, things will look better after a good night's sleep," Jasmine said stretching her arms over her head as Nick drove past the brick pillars that frame the entrance to the Lowe Estate.

"You think so?" Nick asked, sounding doubtful.

"Yes." Jasmine said. "Yes, I do. First, we'll go tell Jaworski what Pete Smith told us, and then we're going to track down Cassie Snyder. All will be well."

Nick leaned forward and peered through the windshield as they approached the house. "Who's that?"

Jasmine squinted as she looked to the front of the mansion. "That's Higgins. Is he pacing?"

Nick let out a small groan. "I don't see Holly's car. This can't be good."

The butler hurried to the car as they pulled up.

"Oh, Ms. Jasmine! You must hurry. Your mother, Miss Ivy, Miss Holly – they only had twenty minutes and they left ten minutes ago."

"Slow down, Higgins," Jasmine said. "Where did they go?"

"Miss Holly said you need to meet them at the bonfire site."

"You know what he's talking about?" Nick asked.

"Yes," Jasmine said.

"Get in the car," Nick ordered. "You, too, Higgins."

Jasmine opened the back door for the butler then quickly got back into the front passenger seat. The moment she closed the door, Nick hit the gas and tore down the long drive back to the main road. Jasmine gave directions as he once again passed the brick pillars.

"Now tell us what happened," Nick said as he pressed down on the accelerator.

"Miss Cassie arrived, and..." Higgins hesitated.

"And what?" Nick asked gruffly, unable to conceal his impatience.

Jasmine turned to face the butler. "Higgins, you need to tell us whatever you know."

"But I'm ... I'm ashamed to admit that I ..."

"Eavesdropped?" Jasmine guessed.

The butler lowered his head. "Yes, I couldn't help myself. I listened outside the door."

"What you heard could save lives, Higgins," Nick said, struggling to remain patient.

The butler lifted his head, "Yes, of course," he said, and proceeded to recount everything from Cassie's arrival up to the departure of the three Donnelly sisters. "I didn't know if calling the police would make things worse, so I just waited for you. I'm sorry if that was wrong."

"It's okay, Higgins," Jasmine said, returning her eyes to the road. "Make a left here, Uncle Nick."

"Call 911," Nick said as he executed the turn.

After Jasmine finished the call, she said, "Maybe you should slow down. The service road entrance isn't too far up ahead. It's just hard to spot."

"No need," Nick replied. "There's Holly's car."

"Oh, great," Jasmine said. "Mom's probably waiting in the car."

Nick brought the Malibu to a stop directly behind Holly's CTS. Jasmine jumped out and ran to the passenger side of the car. Empty.

"Oh no," she said as Nick came up along the driver's side. "I can't believe my mother went with them."

"Seriously?" Nick said. "She's a Donnelly, isn't she?" He clicked the trunk opener on his key fob as he walked back to the Malibu. Reaching in the trunk he inserted a key in what appeared to be a large, black tool box.

"Oh, my!" Higgins gasped as Nick opened the box containing several handguns.

"Expecting a small invasion, Uncle Nick?" Jasmine asked.

Nick didn't reply as he reached for the smallest handgun and chambered a round.

"You know how to use this?" he asked Jasmine.

"Yep," Jasmine reached for the gun. "I took lessons as soon as I started working in the DA's office."

Nick strapped on a shoulder holster, reached for another gun, again chambered a round and slipped it in place. Next, he reached in the trunk and extracted a smaller holster. Lifting his leg, he rested his foot on the back bumper of the car. He attached the second holster to his ankle, grabbed another gun and slid that one in place.

Nick was about to close the trunk when Higgins said, "Sir. I, too, know how to use a gun. I was in the army."

Nick pulled out another handgun from the case and handed it to Higgins. "Whatever you do, don't leave this spot."

Higgins accepted the gun and gave Nick a salute. "Yes sir. Good luck."

Nick turned to Jasmine. "Lead the way."

61 THE TEMPLE

Before they started onto the golf course, Holly and Ivy agreed just how close they would dare to get to the Temple. Close enough to hear what was said, but far enough away not to be noticed in the dark. Ever so slowly, Holly and Ivy inched their way forward. They hadn't reached their desired destination when they saw someone approaching the Temple from the left. Carrying an LED lantern, a hooded figure dressed totally in black appeared and walked up the three steps to the Temple's entrance.

Holly signaled Ivy to sit down in the grass as she removed the fanny pack from her shoulder and placed it on the ground. As she got down on her knees, she had to muster all the self-control she could to keep from yelling 'ouch' when her left knee made contact with a rock. She moved the rock and got into a kneeling position.

Both sisters peered through the branches of their camouflage shrubs but were unable to see exactly what the dark figure was doing. A clanking sound of metal on metal reached their ears, followed by the squeak of the Temple's entrance gate as it opened. Next, they heard metal scraping pavement as the inner door opened outward. The figure left the lantern on the small porch and disappeared inside.

Holly turned to her sister and whispered. "We're in luck. It looks like just one person." Ivy gave a thumbs up in reply.

A gentle whir drew their attention to the golf cart path on the right. The whir grew louder as a golf cart left the paved path and crossed the lawn coming to a stop in front of the Temple. In the dim glow of the lantern, they could see it was Cassie. She got out of the cart clutching her backpack with both arms. Scanning the area, she walked slowly in the direction of the lantern.

"Hello," she called out in a shaky voice. "Mom, are you in there?"

"Shut up," a man's voice commanded. A moment later, Cassie's mother stumbled out onto the small porch of the Temple, propelled by a push from behind.

"Cassie!" she said starting to move forward. Before she took a step, the dark figure grasped her arm, holding her in place.

To Holly's dismay, although the man was now partially in the light of the lantern, the hood still obscured his face. His voice sounded familiar, but she couldn't quite place it.

"I have what you want here in my backpack," Cassie replied.

"Give it to me."

"Let my mother get in the golf cart first."

The man laughed as he pulled out a handgun and aimed it at Cassie. "I'm done wasting time here," he said cocking the trigger.

"Drop your weapon," Holly shouted. In the moment of silence that followed, she connected the two ends of the fanny pack, hoping the sound reached the Temple steps. She peeked through the bushes, slightly amazed to see Ronnie lower his head as he pushed Cassie's mother down the steps, keeping her directly in front of him. Her bluff was working — but for how long?

She turned to Ivy and whispered, "You get ready to move

in the direction of the golf cart."

Ivy nodded, keeping her eyes on the hooded figure.

"Who's there?" the man shouted. "Show yourself or I'll kill these two bitches right now."

"Do it and you're the next body to drop," Holly yelled back. "I've got a 45-magnum pointed at the spot right between your eyes." She picked up the rock she'd nearly kneeled on and signaled Ivy to go. Flinging the rock as hard as she could to her left, she lay down flat on the ground.

A shot rang out. Staying low, Holly turned her head, relieved to see Ivy had managed to move about a foot forward. She raised her head in time to see the hostage and captive descend the steps. Cassie ran to her mother but stopped when Ronnie pointed the gun at her mother's head. He said something Holly couldn't hear. Cassie got in front of him and turned around, grasping her mother's hand.

"We made a copy of the ledger," Holly shouted.

Lying to a criminal wasn't a crime. Nick did it all the time. She instantly regretted it, however, when she saw the man knock Cassie to the ground. Suddenly exposed, the man jerked his head back as he scrambled to get behind her mother. When he did, the hood slid off his head and Ronnie Lowe's face came into full view. Quickly, he crouched down as he pulled the hood back on.

Holly froze in place, not sure whom she expected beneath the hood, but it certainly wasn't Ronnie. She looked to her right. In all the confusion, Ivy had made great progress and was now about fifteen feet from the golfcart. Holly shifted her focus back to Ronnie.

"It's over, Ronnie." Holly shouted. "Peggy talked to your father, and he told her everything."

"You're lying!" Ronnie screamed as he aimed and fired again. Holly lowered her head to the ground as the bullet

whizzed past a few feet to her left. She wondered how long before he accurately gauged where her voice was coming from.
A second shot rang out, forcing her to lower her head to the
ground again as the bullet flew past, closer than the last.

When she raised her head, she saw Cassie getting back on
her feet. Slowly, Ronnie steered Cassie and her mother toward
the golf cart, the women forming a human shield. If Ronnie
managed to get them out of sight, he'd kill them, then come back
for her. She lifted her head to the right.

Oh no! Where's Ivy?

Her sister's shrub seemed to have vanished. She had to do
something. Getting into a squatting position behind her shrub,
Holly began to edge forward. Through the branches she saw
that Ronnie and his hostages had reached the golf cart. Cassie
climbed into the driver's seat. Ronnie stayed crouched behind
her mother, pulling her around to the passenger side. He pushed
her into the seat next to her daughter, then sidled along to the
back of the cart, out of sight.

Holly was now close enough to see Ivy's shrub abandoned
a few feet to the left of the golfcart. What had her sister done?
She didn't have to wait long for an answer.

"What do you mean there's no key?" Ronnie screamed.

62 WARNING SHOT

"I'm not alone, Ronnie," Holly called out. "You're surrounded. The police will be here any minute." She hoped that wasn't a lie.

Ronnie's reply came in the form of another gunshot. Holly sank down realizing her mistake as a bullet tore through the top branches of her shrub. She was too close and now in a better position for Ronnie to pinpoint where her voice was coming from. A dead shrub provided great camouflage, but it would not serve as a protective shield.

Holly kept her head flat waiting for another shot. Nothing. Not a sound for several seconds, until she heard heavy footsteps headed in her direction. Before she could get up, Ronnie was standing over her, his gun pointed directly at her.

"You bitch!" he snarled, grabbing her arm, jerking her to her feet. "I gotta hand it to you. You had me fooled there for a while."

"What gave me away?" she asked.

"You didn't fire once, not even a warning shot," he said, starting to drag her across the grass.

"The police are on their way," Holly bluffed.

"Shut up." He leaned in close to her ear. She could feel his breath on her neck. "There are no police coming and because you can't mind your own business I gotta get rid of three bodies. So you know what? I'm gonna make you watch as I kill those two first." He pointed his gun toward the golf cart.

"What two?" Holly asked.

Ronnie jerked his head and let out a howling scream when he saw the empty golf cart, Cassie and her mother gone. He tightened his grip on Holly, half pushing, half dragging her toward the Temple.

"All right, you bitches," he yelled, placing the barrel of his handgun against the side of Holly's head. "Get your asses back out her where I can see you, or I'm going to kill her right now."

Holly swallowed hard. After just a second, Cassie and her mother appeared from behind the Temple.

"That's better." Ronnie laughed a rather unpleasant laugh and focused a maniacal grin on Cassie. "And I suppose you miraculously found the key, eh?" he said.

Cassie looked stricken. "No." She shook her head. "Honest, I don't know what happened to it. I left it in the ignition when I got here. I don't have it."

Holly glanced sideways, her arm still tightly in Ronnie's grip. She watched his grin turn into an angry grimace. He gave her a hard shake. "So, you weren't lying about not being alone. "Okay," he shouted. "Whoever else is out there, you better show yourself or this one dies first."

"Wait!" a voice came from behind the Temple. Ivy walked out, her hands over her head, the golf cart key dangling from her right hand.

Ronnie pushed Holly towards Cassie. He walked over to Ivy, took the key and waved the gun, motioning her to join them. He aimed the gun at them, but remained still, appearing lost in thought.

"You can't kill all of us and think you're going to get away with this," Holly said.

Ronnie stared at her and after a moment nodded, the maniacal smile returning. "You're right. Now, I want you all to walk over there and up the steps. Nice and slow. The Temple won't be used again for months. By then, you'll all be ..." He let out his unpleasant laugh again. "Well, you know. The good news, no bullets to be traced, no bodies to be disposed of."

As they turned and headed to the Temple steps, Holly asked. "Since we're all dead women, will you at least tell us why you killed Hiram?"

"You're the brainiac," Ronnie said. "Why do you think?"

"I think he figured out you were padding contractor and supplier invoices and pocketing the money, not to mention blackmailing people and laundering that money through the Country Club treasury."

"Oh, hell no," Ronnie jeered. "He thought it was Locksley. And you know why?"

"Why?"

"Because that's how I set it up to look. I was monitoring the books for my father when I discovered that Locksley had a little kickback scheme going — nothing big. I confronted him and he said he'd cut me in." Ronnie laughed. "Generous of him, huh? Of course, I took his small-time operation to a whole other level. It was a thing of beauty, barely detectable, and there was nothing to implicate me." Ronnie's bragging tone quickly turned vicious. "Until Locksley got greedy and started submitting his own set of false invoices. They were so obvious even this stupid girl figured it out and told Hiram."

The women stopped when they reached the Temple porch.

"What are you waiting for, ladies? Step inside your — uh — final resting place."

Ivy led the way in, Cassie and her mother following. Holly hesitated. "What about the blackmailing?"

"Enough!" Ronnie pushed Holly inside. Ivy caught her before she stumbled to the floor. The door creaked, and the room grew darker as Ronnie began to close the door. Before shutting it completely, he leaned in grinning. "See you on the other ..."

A loud cracking sound interrupted his parting words, and Ronnie crashed to the floor.

63 WHAT TOOK YOU SO LONG?

"Get the gun!" Fern yelled, holding the umbrella over her head, poised to strike again.

As Ivy pushed open the door to let in what little light the LED lantern provided, Holly located the gun. Ronnie stirred and started to get up.

Fern delivered a forceful kick to his ribs. "Ah ah ah!" she said as he groaned and curled into a fetal position. "Stay right where you are."

Cassie helped her mother up and they followed Ivy out onto the porch and down the steps. Holly stood up, aiming the gun at Ronnie.

"Go on out, Fern. Get ready to close the door and lock it," Holly said. Fern lowered the umbrella. After she exited, Holly stepped over Ronnie and backed out onto the porch. As soon as she was safely out, Ivy and Fern pushed the door shut, closed the outer gate, and locked the lock.

The three sisters sank down on the top step.

Holly let out a loud sigh and looked at Fern. "Didn't I tell you not to leave the car?" she asked, her lips slowly curling upward.

"You're not the boss of me," Fern quipped, struggling not

to grin.

Seated in the middle, Ivy put her arms around them both and laughed. "I'm just glad you found the umbrella we left behind once we decided to use the shrubs as camouflage."

"Yeah, now you see how useful an umbrella can be?" Holly grinned.

"I'll give you that. When I picked it up and felt the hardness of the handle, I knew it could do some damage." Fern chuckled. "But that window scraper? C'mon. You couldn't hurt a fly with that."

As the sisters laughed, Cassie looked up from the bottom step where she and her mother sat. "You three are amazing. I don't know how to thank you. If it weren't for you, he would have killed us. I'm so sorry for ..."

The sound of approaching footsteps cut her off. Still holding the gun, Holly lifted it skyward, fired a warning shot, then pointed the gun in the direction of the footsteps.

"Aunt Holly, put the gun down! It's us."

Nick jogged into view first, Jasmine close behind.

"What took you so long?" Holly asked.

Nick shook his head. "You want to tell us what happened here."

"All you really need to know is that Ronnie Lowe is locked inside the Temple," Fern said.

"Ronnie?" Jasmine appeared surprised.

"Yes," Cassie replied. "He actually bragged to us that he was the mastermind behind the embezzled funds, and he also said he ..." Cassie choked up, unable to finish her thought.

Cassie's mother put an arm around her and said, "He killed Hiram. And he would have killed us, too, if it hadn't been for them." She pointed her thumb behind her to where the three

Donnellys sat smiling.

Holly grinned at Nick. "That about sums it up."

Before he could reply, everyone turned toward the sound of footsteps once again headed their way. Nick drew the gun from his shoulder holster before Holly even picked hers up.

"Is everyone all right?" Higgins asked as he emerged from the darkness.

Nick sighed, lowering his gun. "Didn't I tell you to … Oh, why bother?" He waved his arm in disgust. As he reholstered his gun, the sound of sirens reached them.

Two police cars arrived first, followed by an unmarked car and an ambulance. Lights from the vehicles brightened the entire area in front of the Temple. Nick headed over when he saw Detective Jaworski get out of the unmarked car.

Holly yawned. "I'm tired."

"I'm hungry," Ivy said.

Fern nodded. "I could eat."

Jasmine shrugged. "I could go for a beer."

Higgins smiled and pulled out his cellphone. "I'll call Mrs. Higgins. Let her know we're all right and we'll be coming home hungry and thirsty."

.

64 POST-MORTEM

Out on the patio, the next morning, Holly and Ivy sat on either end of the wicker couch facing the great lawn of the Lowe Estate. With everyone else sleeping late, they enjoyed the quiet, lingering over their coffee.

"It's so beautiful and peaceful here this morning," Holly said as she finished what was in her mug. "But I have to say, I'll be happy to get back home."

"Me too," Ivy smiled. "But admit it. Aren't you glad I talked you into coming?"

"Yes, I suppose I am," Holly said. "We now have our sister back."

"And two glorious nieces," Ivy grinned. "I can't wait to meet Violet's children. She said she wants to plan a Fourth of July reunion in Florida. You think you and Nick can make it?"

"We'll see. After these few days, he may not be too eager to get together with our side of the family so soon."

"Hey, after our experience with his family in Tuscany, this was a walk in the park." Ivy giggled. "Neither one of you got shot."

Holly let out a belly laugh. "You know, you're right. Maybe

everybody has a murderer in their family tree."

"Good morning," a smiling Peggy said as she joined them. She sat down between her cousins and took each by the hand. "I don't know how I can ever repay ..."

"Stop right there," Holly said. "Don't even use that word when you talk to us."

"Yeah, Peggy." Ivy squeezed her hand. "We're family. You don't need to repay family."

"Nevertheless," Peggy smiled, "I was just on the phone with Charles. The treasure hunt money ..."

"About that ..." Holly sat up. "Look, Ivy and I discussed it. We don't feel comfortable taking your money."

Peggy grimaced. "Too bad. The money's already been transferred to your bank accounts."

"Peggy!" Ivy began to protest.

Peggy stood up. "You can spend it, or you can donate it to your favorite charity if that's what you choose, but I don't want to hear another word about it."

"About what?" Fern asked stepping through the French doors to join them.

Peggy turned to face Fern. "I just told them the treasure hunt money has been deposited in each of your accounts."

"Yes, I called my bank and they told me it was received." Fern stared at Peggy for a moment. "Thank you, Peg. You know, I never wanted this money for myself."

Peggy frowned waggling her head. "As I just told them, I don't want to hear another word about the money. I have more money than I'll ever spend in my lifetime. You all being here, supporting me, putting yourselves in danger for me ..."

"We weren't really in danger," Holly interrupted.

"That's not what Higgins told me," Peggy said.

"I didn't take him for a snitch," Fern said, nestling into one of the wicker armchairs.

"Hi all," Jasmine's cheerful voice called out as she stepped outside. "Good news. Locksley's agreed to turn state's evidence and Ron's been released."

"Oh, that's great," Peggy said, sitting down on the loveseat, patting the adjoining cushion for Jasmine to join her. Her face suddenly reflected concern. "What about Ronnie?"

"He's lawyered up," Jasmine replied. "I'm sure he'll plead not guilty, but I think there's just way too much evidence against him. When his lawyers have a chance to review it all, he'll probably take a plea."

"And what about the Brothers of the Blaze?" Holly asked.

Jasmine smirked. "They're all being questioned as we speak. To be honest, I think a few of them were true believers that the Brotherhood was going to do great things for humanity, sort of like the Shriners. They carried out whatever task Locksley gave them, like recruiting new members and soliciting donations. They may not have even realized that some of the so-called donations they were collecting were actually blackmail payoffs. Jaworski will have to sort them out from the few who themselves were victims of blackmail."

"What I want to know is how they're going to decipher the initials in the ledger," Fern said, sitting down on the couch opposite her sisters.

Jasmine smiled. "That's where Locksley's going to be of most value as a witness. He's agreed to identify and explain all of the information in the ledger. His lawyer, of course, is going to argue that Ronnie coerced him into doing it."

"Is that true?" Ivy asked.

"Pretty much," Jasmine replied. "The Supreme Commander hasn't revealed exactly what Ronnie had on him, but he will if it reduces his sentence. And even though he benefited financially from the whole kickback/blackmail scheme, his law-yer will say he was a victim of extortion. In the end, his co-operation with deciphering the ledger will earn him some points with the judge, I'm sure."

"Is it me, or did that ledger surprise you?" Holly asked. "I mean, it didn't look anything like a ledger. Fern, didn't you say you had a diary that looked like it?"

Fern nodded.

"I was thinking about that too," Ivy said. "Ronnie being a millennial, I would have expected him to use computers to track things. You know, keep everything on a thumb drive."

"Well, I gotta hand it to him," Jasmine said. "He really is an evil genius. That ledger was the only evidence of what was going on. By the way, Locksley thought he had the only key to the file drawer, which is why he kept the ledger there at the Country Club. Anyway, Ronnie had Locksley make all the entries. If any-one found it, first of all, the book itself looked totally innocuous, and if they opened it, they wouldn't know what to make of it. That's why even though Hiram discovered the ledger, he didn't turn it over to the police. He didn't know what it was until Cassie brought those invoices to his attention. That's when he got sus-picious and came to Ron."

Peggy's face reflected deep sadness. "I think that morning we went to Nay Aug, Hiram came to meet with us to give Ron a chance to own up to whatever was going on. I truly believe that if Ron admitted to skimming, then Hiram would have given him a chance to repay the money without ever going to the police."

"But Ron couldn't do that because he didn't know what his son was doing," Jasmine said. "And again, that was part of Ronnie's genius. He had access to the Club's finances through his father. We're not sure at this point, but we think Ronnie may ac-tually have been doing the monitoring his father was supposed to do as Treasurer, which is why he was able to launder the blackmail money through the Club's bank account. At any rate, if any questions arose, then the ledger implicated Locksley and the Club's accounting records implicated Ron."

"What a truly awful person he is," Ivy said. "How could he do that to his own father?"

"In the end, Ron was an unwitting dupe in the whole scheme," Holly said. "Hey, one thing I want to know is if they figured out where Hiram was murdered before the body was brought here."

"Well, they've sent a forensics team to Ron and Beverly's house this morning," Jasmine replied. "They checked the GPS on Hiram's car, and it looks as though he went there after he left here the morning we went to Nay Aug. That's why they thought Ron murdered him."

"But then why did Ronnie murder Hiram?" Ivy asked.

"We don't know for sure yet," Jasmine replied. "Since Ronnie was willing to throw his father under the bus every step of the way, we don't think it was to protect him. Still, Ronnie may have just wanted to stop the audit Hiram was proposing. It's also possible that after meeting with Don, Peggy and Ron, that Hiram believed Ron wasn't involved. He may have had his suspicions about Ronnie and went to the house to talk to him after that meeting."

"But why did Ronnie bring the body here?" Fern asked. "Even if he killed Hiram in his own house, why didn't he just dump it in the woods somewhere?"

"I think I know why," Holly volunteered. "Being the megalomaniac that he is, I suspect he wanted to move to this house as much as Beverly and Ron did. He probably figured putting the body here would scare Peggy into letting them move in."

"Oh my goodness!" Ivy leaned forward and looked directly at Peggy who sat silently throughout the discussion. "He must be the one who fired the shot at you on your balcony."

Peggy's eyes teared up. "I just don't believe Ronnie would

try to kill me."

"I don't think he did," Holly said. "Nick told us he thought that whoever fired that shot missed on purpose. He was just trying to scare you."

"I hate to say this, but if he did take that shot, then he probably planted the gun in Pat's truck too," Jasmine said.

Fern slapped the wicker chair arm. "I'll bet you Beverly gave him that idea. That would kill two birds with one stone. Divert suspicion from her son and eliminate Pat as a prospect for Peggy." Turning to Jasmine, she asked, "Can she be charged as an accessory to the crime?"

"Well, if what you suggest is true, then yes," Jasmine replied. "I'll tell Uncle Nick to mention it to Jaworski. After last night, they're best buddies."

"Hey, speaking of Beverly," Ivy said, her brow furrowed, "why do you think she alerted us to the financial irregularities in the first place? I mean, if she was trying to protect her son, then why would she even let us know something was going on?"

"Good question," Jasmine said. "Uncle Nick thinks that at the point she came here to drop her little hint, she and Ronnie thought they could pin all the financial crimes on Locksley and Ron, diverting all suspicion away from him. They knew Ron wouldn't turn on his son and I guess with whatever they had on Locksley, if it came to his word against Ronnie's, then they felt pretty confident a jury would believe Ronnie's side of the story."

"And with Pat framed for the murder, Ronnie would be home free," Holly added. "By the way, where is Nick?"

Jasmine gave her a sly smile. "Oh, he had to make a stop." Glancing at her watch, she said, "He should be here any minute."

"Oh, this is where you all are," Violet said, stepping onto the patio. "What did I miss?"

Jasmine groaned. "Short answer, Ron's free, Ronnie's in

jail, and Locksley's turned state's evidence."

"That's all good, right?" Violet asked.

"Well, not all good," Peggy frowned.

"Peggy," Nick's voice called from the doorway.

Everyone turned to face him.

"Hope you don't mind, but I brought a guest." Nick stepped onto the patio, Pat Keefe behind him.

65 CELEBRATION

Holly walked over to where Nick was standing at the edge of the patio, looking out at the great lawn. She handed him a champagne flute.

"I think we should stay the night and leave early tomorrow," she said.

Nick nodded, clinking his glass against hers, taking a sip.

"You didn't get any sleep last night, did you?" she asked.

Nick just shrugged.

"Are you speaking to me?"

Letting out a loud sigh, Nick put his free arm around her shoulder. "You know, your family ..."

"Just hold on one minute," Holly smiled. "I have two words for you. *Famiglia* Manelli."

"Touché." Nick said and took a longer swallow of champagne.

"Look, I'm sorry we left the house last night, but ..."

"You didn't have a choice," Nick finished her sentence. "If you hadn't, Cassie and her mother would be dead, and we wouldn't be celebrating with champagne right now."

Holly's eyes widened in amazement. "Did you just admit I

did the right thing?"

"God help me — yes," Nick drank down what remained in his champagne glass.

Holly rested her glass on a nearby table, put her arms around Nick's waist and grinned. "I have never loved you more than at this moment."

"But you know, if you had called me the minute that Hiram's body was discovered ..."

Holly stood on her tiptoes and gave Nick a long, slow kiss.

"You know, I noticed that you do that more and more," Nick said.

"What's that?" Holly asked.

"You kiss me when I'm trying to make a point."

"Well, you do know that I learned that from you, *Amore Mio*." Holly waggled her head.

"I suppose there are worse ways to end an argument." Nick pulled her close and kissed her again.

Holly glanced across the patio in time to see Georgette and Don arrive.

"Welcome home," a smiling Peggy shouted, standing next to Pat. "Come join the celebration."

"What are you celebrating?" Georgette asked.

"Yeah, did we miss anything while we were gone?" Don asked.

As the roar of laughter filled the air, Nick leaned close to Holly and whispered. "I think I need to get some sleep. Care to come upstairs and tuck me in, *Cara Mia*?"

Holly's eyes widened again, this time with delight. "*Si, Amore Mio*. With pleasure."

ACKNOWLEDGEMENT

Thank you to Nina Augello, my alpha reader, who cheers me on when I am in despair and ready to give up.

Thanks to Steve Miller, beta reader and proof-reader non-pareil, and one of the best Holly & Ivy fansI could ask for.

Thanks also to JoAnne Scuderi for her editing expertise (https://www.scuderi.us/) and her appreciation of my English teacher allusions.

Once again Carol Monahan, graphic artist extraordinaire, has exceeded my expectations with a gorgeous cover. Carol consistently translates my ideas into images. (www.carolmonahandesign.com)

I also owe a special debt of gratitude to my Cozy Mystery critique partners whose genuinely constructive critiques and suggestions make me a better writer:

- Judy Buch (www.judybuch.com/)
- Cindy Blackburn (cueballmysteries.com)
- Wayne Cameron, author of the Melvin Motorhead Series (available on Amazon)

Finally, thanks to Sisters in Crime (Sistersincrime.org), both the national and my Upstate South Carolina Chapter (sincupstatesc.blogspot.com) and Malice Domestic (malicedomestic.org). I appreciate the many kindred souls these organizations have linked me with, both published and unpublished writers, who constantly amaze me with their generosity of spirit and willingness to share their knowledge and experience.

ABOUT THE AUTHOR

Sally Handley

Author of the Holly and Ivy Mystery Series, Sally Handley is an avid reader and has been a mystery lover since she read her first Nancy Drew and Trixie Belden books as a young girl. After a career in teaching and marketing, she now devotes her time to writing and gardening. Past President of the Sisters in Crime Upstate SC Chapter, Sally  also co-writes a Kindle Vella series, The Adventures of Trixie with her dog Trixie, and a blog entitled "On Writing, Reading and Retirement" at www.sallyhandley.com.

THE HOLLY AND IVY MYSTERY SERIES

Holly and Ivy Donnelly are middle-aged sisters and avid gardeners. At the start of the series, they're both at a stage in life when they are feeling vulnerable about the aging process. As a result of being drawn into murder investigations, both sisters find inner strength, renewed purpose and romance, experiencing a renaissance at an age when many choose to accept the limitations of aging. Holly and Ivy may not have superpowers, but their unique life experience helps them to help others.

Second Bloom

Holly Donnelly, an adjunct English professor, and her younger sister, Ivy Donnelly, a recently widowed, retired nurse are reluctantly drawn into the investigation of an elderly neighbor's murder when Juan Alvarez, Holly's trusted gardener, is accused of the crime. Holly fears police detective, Nick Manelli, assumes Juan is guilty and won't conduct a proper investigation, while Ivy feels the "hunky" Manelli is not only a good cop, but also a possible romantic match for her sister. Can the clues the sisters unearth from neighborhood gossip about the victim's family, a politically connected neighbor and a powerful real estate developer help save an innocent man, or will the gardening duo dig up more than they bargain for?

Frost On The Bloom

In Frost on the Bloom, the second in the Holly & Ivy mystery series, one of Holly's former students, Becky Powell, asks the look-alike sisters for help when they all spend Christmas at Skyview Manor, and Becky becomes the prime suspect in the attempted murder of her manipulative grandmother, Lyla Powell. Once again the plucky sisters are reluctantly drawn into a murder investigation, convinced that Mrs. Powell's duplicitous friends and greedy Powell family members have framed Becky for the crime. Holly's involvement becomes a source of contention between her and Detective Nick Manelli, threatening their budding romance. Can their relationship continue to sizzle as the investigation heats up and the sister sleuths try to catch a cold-blooded killer?

Full Bloom

Looking forward to a relaxing stay in the Catskills after her break-up with Nick Manelli, Holly Donnelly and her sister Ivy have their plans thwarted when, once again, they become involved in a murder investigation. The day they arrive at Kate Farmer's house in rustic Reddington Manor, they discover the body of Kate's next-door neighbor, Chuck Dwyer, in a pool of blood on his kitchen floor. In a rush to judgement, the local sheriff sets his sights on 17-year old Tommy Cranston, but Kate insists Tommy is innocent. Can the sister sleuths prove that a shifty neighbor, the victim's widow and local drug dealers all have better motives for the murder? And can Ivy and Kate unravel another mystery -- the cause of Holly and Nick's break-up and the chances of their getting back together?

Murder Under Tuscan Blooms

The Manelli family vineyard in Tuscany seems the perfect spot for Holly and Nick's honeymoon, until the suspicious death of a long-lost cousin who's come to stake a claim on the vineyard. Plans for a marriage celebration are thrown into disarray as Holly, Nick and their extended family are drawn into the investigation. Was it an accident or was it murder? Will they solve the mystery, or is the honeymoon over?

BOOKS BY THIS AUTHOR

Stop The Threat

When a small-town arms its teachers, they think they've found the answer to improving school security. School Resource Officer Jeff Stone must implement the new gun-carry policy he opposes. English teacher Ellen McCall has reasons for not wanting to carry a gun, reasons she hopes to keep buried in the past. The pair find themselves embroiled in controversy when the policy divides the town and triggers a series of events, both unexpected and deadly.

Made in United States
North Haven, CT
16 February 2022